"ARE YOU AFRAID OF ME, CELESTE?"

The old gypsy beckoned her forward. "Don't hang back. Why, I am too weak to hurt anyone."

But the power in her eyes belied her words, and for a moment Celeste was afraid to move. Then she told herself she was being a fool. After all, Dron was here to protect her, and he was as big as any man on Nov except for Boris. Celeste took a step forward.

But the old woman was gazing past her now, impaling Dron on a stare. He screamed and covered his face as the gypsy began to chant in Romany.

Then, fearing her magic, petrified by thoughts of the evil eye, he let out a cry of terror and fled. Celeste, too, tried to escape. But she was surrounded by gypsies, and as a cloth soaked in chloroform came down over her face, she plunged into empty blackness. . . .

Other SIGNET Gothics You'll Want to Read

- MANSION IN MINATURE by Elizabeth St. Clair. (#W7409—$1.50)
- ☐ STONEHAVEN by Elizabeth St. Clair. (#Q5946—95¢)
- ☐ THE BROKEN KEY by Mary Linn Roby. (#Y6766—$1.25)
- ☐ SIGNET DOUBLE GOTHIC—THIS LAND TURNS EVIL SLOWLY by Mary Linn Roby and DIG A NARROW GRAVE by Mary Linn Roby. (#J8131—$1.95)
- ☐ SIGNET DOUBLE GOTHIC—THE WHITE PEACOCK by Mary Linn Roby and SHADOW OVER GROVE HOUSE by Mary Linn Roby. (#J7893—$1.95)
- ☐ A HAUNTED PLACE by Virginia Coffman. (#W7934—$1.50)
- ☐ THE HIGH TERRACE by Virginia Coffman. (#W8228—$1.50)
- ☐ ISLE OF THE UNDEAD by Virginia Coffman. (#W8032—$1.50)
- ☐ NIGHT AT SEA ABBEY by Virginia Coffman. (#W8093—$1.50)
- ☐ DARK CITADEL by Caroline Farr. (#Y7552—$1.25)
- ☐ HOUSE OF VALHALLA by Caroline Farr. (#W8130—$1.50)
- ☐ SIGNET DOUBLE GOTHIC—A CASTLE IN SPAIN by Caroline Farr and SO NEAR AND YET . . . by Caroline Farr. (#E8057—$1.75)
- ☐ SINISTER HOUSE by Caroline Farr. (#W7892—$1.50)
- ☐ HERMITAGE HILL by Dorothy Daniels. (#W8092—$1.50)
- ☐ CASTLEREAGH by Monica Heath. (#W8056—$1.50)
- ☐ DUNCRAIG by Monica Heath. (#W7935—$1.50)
- ☐ MARSHWOOD by Monica Heath. (#W7801—$1.50)

THE NEW AMERICAN LIBRARY, INC.,
P.O. Box 999, Bergenfield, New Jersey 07621

Please send me the SIGNET BOOKS I have checked above. I am enclosing $__________(check or money order—no currency or C.O.D.'s). Please include the list price plus 35¢ per copy for postage and handling. Prices and numbers are subject to change without notice.

Name______________________________

Address____________________________

City______________State__________Zip Code__________

Allow at least 4 weeks for delivery

THE JEWELED SECRET

by
Elizabeth St. Clair

A SIGNET BOOK
NEW AMERICAN LIBRARY
TIMES MIRROR

NAL BOOKS ARE ALSO AVAILABLE AT DISCOUNTS IN BULK QUANTITY FOR INDUSTRIAL OR SALES-PROMOTIONAL USE. FOR DETAILS, WRITE TO PREMIUM MARKETING DIVISION, NEW AMERICAN LIBRARY, INC., 1301 AVENUE OF THE AMERICAS, NEW YORK, NEW YORK 10019.

SIGNET, SIGNET CLASSICS, MENTOR, PLUME AND MERIDIAN BOOKS
are published by The New American Library, Inc.,
1301 Avenue of the Americas, New York, New York 10019

FIRST SIGNET PRINTING, AUGUST, 1978

1 2 3 4 5 6 7 8 9

PRINTED IN THE UNITED STATES OF AMERICA

In memory of Indigo and Monday:
my beautiful Russian Blue cats

THE JEWELED SECRET

Chapter I

Celeste Dorchester stared at the magnificent diamond. Seeing it here at the 1927 Paris Exhibition of World-Famous Jewels, no one would ever guess what a dangerous stone it was, a source of treachery, a cause of death. As if she were a little girl looking into the window of a sweet-shop, she pressed her face to the glass which separated her from the gem. She loved jewels with a passion. And now she was gazing at the wonder of them all, the absolute star of the exhibition.

She could barely believe that at last she was this close to the Azov Diamond, Count Dimitri Azov's gift to his mistress and empress, Catherine the Great, in 1768. Celeste wanted the diamond. She'd never before seen anything she wanted so much. Caught up, dazzled, she didn't notice the man standing a few feet away, watching her intently. A tall man with dark hair, he was the equal of any silent film star or matinee idol for looks. But he was so obviously bold and arrogant that he seemed more pirate than stage hero.

He watched the girl coveting the diamond and thought to himself that she was right to want it. She was so extraordinarily beautiful that she was the only woman he'd ever seen who could wear it without being eclipsed by it.

What a gem! A 45 karat brilliant-cut indigo stone, whose facets flashed rainbows of fire. But that girl staring at it was a bit of a jewel herself. He shifted his attention to her again. She had eyes the color of sapphires and skin which showed the glow of a polished pearl. Her unrouged cheeks were garnet. No stick of colored wax, that awful stuff which had just become fashionable, was needed to turn her mouth to ruby.

She had to be French. The man was sure of it. Look how she'd wrapped that blue scarf around her throat so that it seemed to caress her. And the little hat—why, it sat jauntily over the bobbed hair. What color was the hair? Not gold, not brown, a bit of either depending on the light. Now he had it. The hair was amber.

He approached her, cutting through the crowd, then spoke to her in French. "The diamond's not for sale."

She laughed a little bitterly and answered, "Do I look as if I could buy it?" Her French was flawless.

"You look rich enough to buy the moon."

"Not a slice of it."

"What? I don't believe it."

"I've had my ups and downs," she admitted.

"And I take it this is a down."

"A long one," she said sadly. "Very long."

"Too bad you can't have the diamond then. It would solve all your problems. You could sell it to an Indian raja and buy yourself a castle in Spain, a Rolls-Royce, a yacht, and a pied-à-terre here in Paris."

He'd catalogued her wishes. She stopped looking at the diamond and looked at him. He was superb, a Rudolph Valentino type with sleek black hair. But he was frightening. Even if he tried, he couldn't disguise the rather sinister quality of his face.

"Are you a jewel thief?" she asked.

He was startled. "What makes you say that?"

"The greedy way you look at the diamond."

He laughed, it seemed to her, ironically.

She went on. "Well, you must have some source for your money, and I can't believe it's anything mundane as, say, banking."

"What makes you think I have money?"

"You're wearing a well-cut suit. Your shirt's silk, and silk is expensive." What she thought but didn't dare say was that no man's body was ever so beautifully formed unless he had leisure time. Instead, she told him, "You do what you please. Ride horses, play tennis, swim. You live idly—don't you—and elegantly, and that takes cash."

"Would you believe me if I told you I was poor?" he said.

"No."

"Then why should I believe you when you tell me you have no money?"

Touché.

"Not that it matters," he said. "Rich or poor, we're two of a kind."

Oh, no. He sensed what she couldn't deny: that she'd inherited her father's love of adventure, his craving for excitement. This man standing beside her who reminded her so much of a black-haired Viking was, in fact, very like her father. She'd developed a sixth sense about such men. She'd avoid him. Precisely because she was attracted to him, he was all wrong.

She turned her full attention to the diamond.

"Forget it," the man urged. "Though it would seem to have very little to do with socialism, the Russians are very attached to it."

"Yes, I know."

"Its whole history?" he asked.

"Much of it."

"I thought you would. Obviously you're a connoisseur."

"Hardly that. Only an amateur," and she added softly, "for the time being."

The crunch of people around the diamond was growing worse. A rich scent of perfume rose from the enveloping crowd. As he was pushed toward Celeste, his hand accidentally brushed against her hair. As he'd expected, its texture was as sensuous as silk.

She pulled away from him. "I know that the diamond belonged originally to the shah of Persia," she said.

"That was later."

"Thieves killed the shah to get it."

"Naturally. Who can blame them?"

"I ought to say you can't mean that, but I know perfectly well that you do."

"Don't be a hypocrite. You'd do anything you could to own that stone."

She sighed. "Probably. No wonder it's left such a legacy behind it. Death. Intrigue."

"Yes. Men have lusted after it since it was taken from the Golconda mine in India in the fifteenth century. Women, too, apparently, since it was the shah's own concubine who killed him over the jewel. She died, too, in her turn. Murdered by a harem eunuch who sold it."

"How could anyone sell it?"

"You would have kept it?"

"Naturally."

"Even though it was worth a fortune even then?"

"It's priceless."

"Oh, you are caught. Good thing then that you don't own it. It would corrupt you. The eunuch wasn't sentimental. When he sold the diamond to a Syrian merchant, he became a rich man. The merchant was killed, too."

For a moment they watched the diamond in silence. It sparkled innocently.

"After that it vanished," the man said. "Then in the eighteenth century Count Dimitri Azov learned that there was a fabulous diamond kept in a temple in northern China. Who knows how many hands it had passed through along the way, how many more deaths and betrayals it had caused? Azov sent a Turkish thief to steal it. A dangerous mission. Do you know how the thief pulled it off?"

"No."

"He cut a deep gash in his thigh, put the diamond inside the gash, and then sewed the two halves of the wound together."

Celeste gasped.

"Gruesome but effective. The thief smuggled the jewel across the border and presented it to Count Azov. Catherine the Great was delighted with the gem and rewarded the count with a very large estate in return."

"She placed it in the tip of her royal scepter," said Celeste. "I don't think any stone has had quite such an honor."

"And the diamond found peace at last. It was taken out on state occasions. Otherwise it was kept in the diamond room of the Winter Palace in St. Petersburg."

"And it weathered the Revolution."

"Yes, got through 1917 with all its disruption and looting. Of course, the Bolsheviks did consider selling it when they came to power."

"But they didn't."

"It would be like selling a piece of Russia. The jewel is a symbol, an emblem, a part of history, a national treasure."

"We're lucky to see it."

"Its first time out of Russia. But tomorrow it goes home to the Kremlin," he said regretfully. Then as if teasing, he added, "Why don't you pretend you're a representative of the Soviet government come to retrieve it? Charm the guards into giving it to you."

"I suspect they're invulnerable to charm. Besides, I don't speak Russian."

"No reason for you to speak anything but French. You are so obviously, mademoiselle, a Parisienne."

She swung around then, turned her head up, and looked at him. He appraised her: the slim neck, a graceful pedestal for her head; the perfect oval of her face and the charming lift of the chin which finished it. Then the sapphire eyes caught him, looked so deeply into his own that he felt their blue light pierce his heart.

He thought that Cupid had shot him with an arrow.

"I am not French," she said, and he was astonished. "Like you, I'm an American."

"Like me?"

"Yes. You've an American accent."

"And you've none."

"Well, I've been abroad a very long time."

"You surprise me. Come away and we'll dine together. You'll tell me more."

"No," she said firmly.

"Why not?" He wasn't used to being refused.

"For one thing I don't know you. I'm not some lost little soul to be swept up and carried away."

He was about to say that all he'd had in mind was a pleasant evening. But he caught himself, for he realized that "lost" was precisely the word for her. Lost and sad. It didn't show on the glittering surface, but she was vulnerable and lonely.

He was staggered by this insight, for he'd never concerned himself with a woman's motives, her inner self. He felt an unaccustomed tenderness.

"Besides, I haven't time to get to know you," she said. And she added cruelly, "Though even if I had all the years of my life free to give to you, I wouldn't."

He didn't even hear her. He was taken up with his own thoughts. "You've been hurt," he said. "Someone's made you very unhappy. A man?"

"Yes," Celeste said. But what would he think if he knew the man who had hurt her was her father? She'd been only an observer on the sidelines of his life, but that had been enough.

A door opened in her mind, a door leading to a whole corridor of memories. Her father with women, different women, a long line of women. A new love waiting at every grand hotel on the Continent. Tantrums. Reconciliations. Jealous husbands. Threats. And even afterward when the money was gone, he'd still found women, though by then he'd had the good sense to keep his daughter and his mistresses wholly separate.

But when she was a child, she'd had to meet them.

"I must leave now," she said.

"Leave?" He let slip, "But I've just found you."

She meant what she said, took one last look at the diamond, embedding its image in her mind. Other admirers pressed against the glass, enchanted. They had the look of worshipers who have at last reached the goal of their pilgrimage. The Azov Diamond spangled them indiscriminately with its magic light. Their mouths fell open. They exulted.

Celeste wished the jewel a silent good-bye, for when would she ever go to Moscow to see it? Moscow was a cold, impoverished city rocked by a decade of revolution, civil war, and assassination, its gates firmly shut against tourists and bourgeois outsiders. Moscow was night and day different from Paris. And Paris was the city she loved.

"I have no choice, I must go," she said, more to the diamond than the man.

She broke away, moving, as he knew she would, with angelic grace. He followed, catching her at a display of purple amethysts which had belonged to Charlemagne. "I don't know your name or where to find you," he said. "Give me your address, please."

"No." The word clanged like an iron door slamming shut. She was implacable.

"Who are you? At least tell me that much. Look, I'll introduce myself. The name is Nick—"

"There's no time. This is my last day in Paris."

"I'll never forget you," he said. How often had he said that and lied. But he wasn't lying now.

She stared at his pirate's face and wondered what awful things he must have done. And blamed herself for being drawn to him, wondering what was the matter with her that she invariably liked evil and violent men.

Well, a woman didn't have to follow her instincts.

She smiled once. It was a gesture of farewell. Her smile was beautiful. He reached out toward her, to keep her from leaving. But the crowd, like waves of the sea, poured between them and separated them. He caught sight of her, then lost her.

He reached the street. People leaving the exhibition were strolling along; the rich were getting into cars. Streetlights were lit, for it was already dusk. He looked up and down the street but couldn't find her. She was gone. Vanished into the heart of Paris and by tomorrow would be where?

He got hold of himself. This was no time for romantic nonsense. He was playing for very high stakes. He turned around. There was still time to go back to the exhibition.

Inside, he found two more Soviet guards watching the diamond. It was almost as if they were expecting an eleventh-hour attempt to steal the jewel. He pushed past them.

Then he stood still, just staring at the diamond for a very long time.

Blocks away Celeste walked alone, shivering a little from the autumnal dampness. People turned their heads to stare at her, watching her as long as they could until she vanished, like a star when morning comes.

Chapter II

The train was crossing a dull, flat landscape, empty under the vast sky. To beat down the fear of what was awaiting her at the end of the journey, Celeste tried to remember the other trip she'd made across a flat plain. The steppe it was called. The Russian steppe.

Russia. That took Celeste back to her last day in Paris, when she'd seen the Azov Diamond, and to the man who had viewed it with her. Good thing she'd never see him again.

But whom would she see on the estate of the half-mad Russian countess who was waiting for her? Strange people, people a good deal worse than that man.

She clutched the package in her hands tightly.

She hadn't seen Russia since she was eight, when her father took her on that one brief visit. At the thought of her father she felt a chill. It was impossible to think of him without recalling his little cruelties: the way he'd whipped horses even when he'd loved them; his brutality to servants; his daring. Only a daring man would have stolen the package she held so possessively. Of course, he'd told her he'd bought it, but she knew better. There hadn't been any money, and he'd always lied.

And because of that theft, she was on her way to a small Russian enclave. Scant impressions of the real Russia had stayed with her: a river, broad and sluggish; the scent of a pine forest on a summer day. But that wasn't enough. She'd be an outsider.

She shivered slightly. What would the émigrés be like living here, their fortunes gone, their world dead, killed by a revolution? Her father's friends had been exotic enough in their native land.

Celeste looked out the train window. This peaceful American prairie seemed as alien to her as Russia had, for she knew nothing of her own country. She had left it as an infant.

She longed for crowded Europe, for buildings that looked old. The houses on the steppe had been medieval. Her father hadn't liked them. He'd filled her head with stories about the Trans-Siberian Railroad and the Moscow factories which he'd helped finance.

Then came 1917 and the Bolsheviks. The czar was deposed, then killed. Nigel Dorchester lost everything. And because of that, she was now on this train. He'd been dead for precisely six months, and she had nothing of worth except the package. That was her patrimony.

She was twenty-five now, and for close to a decade she had warded off his attempts to marry her to the highest bidder, his only reason for putting up with her. In the end he'd spent most of his time with his last mistress, ignoring his daughter altogether.

Celeste felt tears in her eyes. When she was little, Celeste had prayed that her mother would come and take her away from her father. But her mother hadn't come. She was too busy being the beauty of her day.

After 1917 there was no more alimony, and her mother's looks were going. One morning the news came that she'd taken laudanum. Nigel and Celeste were living in a cheap flat by then.

Celeste never tried to leave. Nigel wouldn't let her. Now she was free of him, alone for the first time in her life. Alone and frightened.

The train was moving due north, and though it was only November, it was bitterly cold. Well, Celeste had been warned that Wisconsin had a long winter. The sky that dominated the prairie was already heavy with snow clouds.

Celeste fumbled with her handbag, a good leather one she'd got on sale. She took out the letter and read it over.

It was from the Countess Helene Ustinova, telling her that she could come to Nov. She could come. The letter did not encourage her, did not make her feel welcome. Yes, the countess indicated, she did remember Celeste's father. Her husband, Count Ustinov, had spoken highly of him. She always did everything she could to help the victims of those terrible Bolsheviks, but usually the victims were Russian.

There was only one line in the letter which glowed with warmth. "I cannot wait to see your precious treasure again."

If it weren't for the package, Celeste thought, the countess probably would have turned her away.

The train stopped. Celeste gathered up her things. She didn't have very much. She'd had to sell almost everything she owned just to raise the fare to come to America. She walked down the aisle, past the one other person in the car, a man asleep with a newspaper over his face. A conductor helped her off the train, staring at her as if he couldn't believe such a vision of loveliness was real.

The train pulled away. A wind blowing free and unrestrained across the prairie made Celeste shiver. She waited a long time and at last saw a speck on the horizon. It was a silver Rolls-Royce, the sort of car she could step into with ease, the kind that suited a Dorchester. Once her father had owned a car like that.

Then the car drew close. Celeste recoiled. Instead of the smart chauffeur she'd expected, the man driving the car struck a grim, discordant note. A figure out of old Russia, he was a huge peasant with a black beard. He stared at her in silence from eyes bright and hypnotic.

She crept into the car and let this dreadful Rasputin of a man drive her across the cold Wisconsin prairie. "I'm dreaming," she thought. "This can't be happening. I feel as if a serf is taking me to his master's estate outside Moscow. Yet all around me are normal American farms with white houses and red barns."

There was a blanket for warmth folded neatly on the back seat of the car. Celeste wrapped it around herself.

Then she noticed something embroidered on it, a double-headed eagle, symbol of the Romanov czars.

"I don't understand. There is no czar. He's dead. Old Russia's dead."

They had been driving a long time before Celeste became aware of a subtle change in the landscape. There were no more houses, just farms or perhaps even a single farm, stretching away as far as she could see.

Could the countess possibly be so extraordinarily rich, own so very much land? Was this Nov at last? She leaned forward, but the man behind the wheel was rigid and formidable. She was afraid to ask.

She watched for a house, imagining some great American dwelling place, something with a vast porch and gingerbread trim. Or even a simple frame house writ large. Then in the distance she caught her first glimpse of Nov's center, and her head reeled.

"I don't believe it," she whispered. "*Déjà vu, déjà vu.*"

The car went on. It couldn't be, yet Celeste recalled how she had run to keep up with her father as he crossed these very fields seventeen years before. She knew the thick pine forest that began at the edge of the fields. There ahead was the inevitable village of log houses straight from the taiga, Russia's northern woods. The car hurried past groups of peasants, yes, peasants—not farmers—wearing Russian clothes, old-fashioned clothes.

The road curved, and the car passed a beautiful wooden church with an onion-shaped dome. Celeste had entered that church with her father. She was sure of it. Beggars in rags had swarmed around it, and Gypsies in kerchiefs had stood at its door. They drove past an area of parks and gardens, desolate in the raw cold, and then they arrived at the manor house, overlooking a lake.

Celeste stepped out of the car and stared. She knew it. She'd seen it or a hundred like it scattered over the Russian countryside. Typically it was made of wood. The Russians always built with wood. But also typically it lacked the clarity and integrity of the little church. It was a huge eclectic busybody of a mansion, part French, part Italian, with Turkish tendencies thrown in.

Eccentric, just like the aristocrats themselves.

Inside, Countess Ustinova was waiting for her. Celeste took a deep breath, for she vividly remembered herself entering this house as a child. Followed closely by the bearded peasant, she entered the manor house of Nov.

Chapter III

Celeste stood in the center of a glittering drawing room out of the last century and said in a soft voice, "I remember your husband, Count Ustinov. He took me into this room, told me in French I was charming, and patted me on the head."

Countess Ustinova rose and confronted Celeste. "You were charming. A beautiful child. And of course, the count spoke to you in French. It is the language of the aristocracy. We still speak it here at Nov. Russian is for peasants."

The countess was cold and aloof. But Nigel had said that behind this dignified facade was a woman of mystical dreams, a fanatic. The count had been the practical one. He'd humored her to keep her happy.

But in 1918 the count had died.

"How sad that you aren't Russian," said the countess critically, "and I see you are very modern. I find this jazz age of yours an ugly time. Imagine, flappers doing the Charleston. And the furniture, such flimsy stuff, Bauhaus style they call it. When I was a girl, rooms looked like this."

"I feel as if I'm in Russia again," said Celeste.

"So you are," the countess said with deep satisfaction. "I have had everything rebuilt here exactly as it was in Russia. To me, Nov means 'Virgin soil,' as it did to Turgenev in his great novel, but perhaps I should have named this estate The Phoenix, for it is Old Russia rising again in a new land."

The countess frowned. "Now open your package. I've waited long enough."

Celeste untied the string, opened the box and the box within that. Then she held up her prize.

It was an egg.

"The czarina's Easter egg," the countess cried. "I was there the day the czar presented it to her. That was in 1916. The World War was on. We all were very tense. Czarina Alexandra was exhausted, worn out by everything: her duties, her charities, the little czarevich's illness. Then she saw this and smiled. So the czar praised Fabergé for twenty minutes."

"Peter Carl Fabergé was wonderful, wasn't he? Goldsmith to the crowned heads of Europe," Celeste said.

"He was without equal. Well, who else could have created this?"

Countess Ustinova cupped the egg in her hand. It was only four inches high, but exquisitely made of enameled nephrite. Red as a Chinese lacquered box, it was decorated with garlands of tiny inexpensive rose-cut diamonds. Its only extravagances were five pearl-bordered doors.

"And when you consider," said the countess, "how the czar told Fabergé he must not use expensive materials because of the war, his achievement is all the more remarkable. I remember years when the Easter eggs were made out of gold with splendid surprises hidden inside them. A tiny gold train that ran on a miniature track, an elfin coach trimmed with a diamond crown."

Countess Ustinova went taut. "I remember the surprise in this egg all too well. Show me."

Celeste opened the little doors set around the egg. Behind each was an enameled portrait of one of the czar's children.

"How grim they look," said the countess. "It was the war. To think they are dead, all of them. Shot. Butchered by barbarians, even their little dog."

The countess' coldness had gone. Fury made her eyes bright and forced her mouth into a hard line.

"See how the four girls sat for their portraits in their

nurse's uniforms. And the czarevich in his army uniform. They were conscientious and innocent, my five little doves. I loved them all."

"The girls look so young," Celeste said.

"That is because they were brought up strictly, nurtured and protected for a single purpose: to adorn a throne. And Olga, the eldest, would have been married, too, if it hadn't been for the war. She was twenty-one."

Celeste stared at the fresh, unsophisticated faces.

"Bluebells, daisies, and violets," she said softly.

"What?"

"Sorry, just a line from an old nursery rhyme I was taught as a child."

"Girls like that don't exist anymore," the countess said emphatically. "The Bolsheviks have spread lies about our decadence, but there was nothing decadent about the czar and his family, I assure you. Olga was very sweet. Marie and Anastasia were adorable. The poor czarevich, of course, was a brave boy. You know he was a hemophiliac. A bleeder." The countess crossed herself in Russian style. "I thank God for Rasputin. I do think he was a holy man with great powers who really did help soothe the czarevich."

Celeste saw again the face of the peasant who had driven her to Nov, a man with eyes of flame. She shuddered.

She began closing the little doors in her egg. Then she realized something odd. "What about Tatiana, the czar's second daughter?"

"Tatiana?" The countess sounded wary.

"Yes. You didn't mention her when you described the czar's children. What was she like?"

"Charming," Countess Ustinova said with a flat finality.

Puzzled, Celeste stared at Countess Ustinova for a moment. But she sensed that she'd better ask no further questions.

Abruptly the countess said, "I'll have you shown to your room. You can begin your study of Fabergé tomorrow."

"I'm so glad you let me come," Celeste said. "I know that you have one of the finest collections of his treasures in the world."

"Well, if you're really intent upon opening a shop which specializes in Fabergé someday, then Nov is the right place to start." The countess added, "Though really with your beauty I don't know why you bother. Find yourself a rich husband. It ought to be easy for you."

"No," Celeste said so forcefully that now it was the countess' turn to stare. "I love good things, I won't deny it. I'd like nothing more than to spend my whole life in elegant surroundings."

"The way you used to live when you were a child."

"Yes. But I won't marry for money." She didn't add that her mother had done precisely that—and look what had happened to her. Nor did she tell any stories about her father's mistresses, some of whom he had essentially bought in his richer days. She had seen how their lives had gone.

"I'll wait. I want stability and security."

"Odd words for the daughter of Nigel Dorchester. Wouldn't you be bored with the kind of man who could give you those things? Your father always craved adventure."

"I know what adventure brings in its wake. Misery."

"Misery." The countess' face took on a mournful look. "I have known my share of that. The motherland destroyed, our estates confiscated. I was lucky to escape. Luckily the count had made heavy foreign investments in English railroads and American steel. Otherwise, we would have been poor, like so many of our friends. But the trauma of it all killed my husband. So I began the building of Nov nine years ago. I have brought hundreds out of Russia since." Her face crumpled. "But I was unable to save the czar. No matter what I spent, how I plotted, I was unable to rescue the czar."

"You oughtn't to blame yourself for that. No one could help him." A sudden thought came to Celeste. "That man who brought me here, who is he? Did you rescue him?"

"Dron? No, it was the other way around. When the count and I fled Russia, he came with us. We wore simple peasant clothes, but even so, we were stopped and searched at the border. We had left most of our possessions behind, including our jewels, but we did take one magnificent ruby, for we could not bear to part with such a valuable gem. We were terrified that it would cost us our lives, for Dron had it sewn inside his clothes when we were searched."

"What did you do?"

"I did nothing. Dron swallowed the ruby so the Bolsheviks wouldn't discover it, and we crossed the border without incident."

A man who would swallow a ruby! The countess rang for him. At the sight of Dron Celeste shrank back.

The countess gave him an order in Russian. Then she turned to Celeste. "Go with him," she said. "He will take you to your room. You'll meet my other guests, the émigrés, at dinner."

Celeste forced herself to follow Dron.

"Oh, Celeste?"

"Yes?"

Tentatively the countess asked, "One last thing. Would you consider selling your Easter egg?"

"Sell my Fabergé!" Celeste clutched the little treasure to her heart.

"I'd pay you far more than it's worth. It's not one of his more valuable pieces, you know, not in a class with the pearl necklace he made for Madame Oupenskaya or with his earlier eggs. I want it for its sentimental value."

"But it's to be the basis of my collection. I can't afford to part with it."

"Yes, I see. No, no, don't apologize. I understand."

But the countess sounded exceptionally cold as she said, "Only do be careful and stay at Dron's side. This is a very large house, and I will be very angry with him if you get lost."

"Now what in the world does she mean by that?"

Celeste thought as the bearded servant led her away. "How in the world could I get lost?"

But perhaps it was possible, for Dron kept very close to her as they walked along. Almost as if he were her jailer.

Chapter IV

It was like walking along corridors peopled with ghosts. There wasn't a sound to be heard as émigrés occasionally passed by. They all were old and looked as if they'd stepped out of the past. The interior of the house was magnificent but in a way which reminded Celeste that Russia wasn't Western. Turks and Mongols lived within its borders, and for a long reach its land edged China. She was lost in a corner of the world all its own.

An elderly lady fluttered by, a creature out of a Chekhov story. She stopped and stared at Celeste, bewildered. Two aged generals, remnants of the czar's army in an earlier day, paused as Celeste walked by. She heard them whisper her name and her father's.

"Nominally this is America," Celeste thought, "but actually I might be in the land of the Cossacks or in Vladivostok."

She wished she'd stayed in Paris. She felt vulnerable, on the edge of alarm, wondering what laws applied here, what conventions she didn't understand. Then, with her practiced eye, she caught sight of an extraordinary malachite vase nine feet high at the end of an adjoining corridor.

"Oh," she cried, "how remarkable!" And drawn as she was to all minerals and gems, she veered instinctively and hurried toward it.

To her amazement the peasant Dron was upon her with a roar, grabbing her and whirling her around.

"Let go of me!"

He stood mute and hostile.

And Celeste heard clearly and distinctly the sound of a girl crying behind one of the closed doors.

"Who's crying?"

With startling abruptness the crying stopped. A door opened.

Dron said something sharply and let go of Celeste. She spun around, thinking she'd see some poor weeping girl. Instead, she found herself staring at a middle-aged woman.

"Well, why are you staring at me like that?" the woman asked in a rough, gravelly voice.

The woman presented the most astonishing sight Celeste had ever seen. She was as flamboyant as a Gypsy and wore a rainbow of colors. Yet her dress was disgustingly dirty. She was enormously fat with bulbous features and double chins so that at first glance she was almost comical. But her clear blue eyes were shrewd and forceful.

"Who are you, and what are you doing here with Dron?" she asked, lighting a cigarette.

She had the hands of a chain smoker, nicotine embedded in the skin. Defiantly she wore a bright cheap ring on every finger.

"Never mind," she amended. "I can guess. You are that Dorchester girl."

"And who are you?" Celeste couldn't help asking as she took in the hair, gray and woolly like a sheep's, the brooches pinned helter-skelter over the front of her dress. A female fool left over from the Romanov court? An old family retainer too poor to dismiss?

"I am Madame Natalia Kropotkina."

What a funny name, like Kropotkin, the famous anarchist.

"Why did you come this way? Your room is at the other end of the house."

"I just wanted to have a look at this vase."

"Well, now that you've seen it perhaps you'll leave."

"I thought—"

"You thought what?"

"That I heard a girl crying."

Madame Kropotkina's face lost every bit of expression. "You heard nothing," she said.

"But I know I did."

"Voices carry at Nov."

Celeste looked around her at walls solidly built and knew the woman lied. But she had no intention of arguing, not with Dron standing there, scowling.

Madame Kropotkina stayed where she was, watching carefully as Celeste went back the way she'd come. Just before Dron hurriedly moved Celeste away, she heard one more sound. She would have sworn it was the mewing of a cat.

Dron left her at the door of her room. She was shaken by her meeting with the outlandish Madame Kropotkina, by the crying she'd heard. Yet she responded immediately to the luxury of her surroundings. The room was too baroque for her taste, but it was good to have lovely things again. The bedspread was the finest of satins, and the Oriental carpet beneath her feet was bright with woven color.

The small amount of luggage she'd brought had arrived, and a maid was already busily unpacking. Celeste took her precious Easter egg and set it on top of a dresser. With its bright red glow, its pearls and tiny diamonds, it merged with the decor, but as far as Celeste was concerned, it became the room's centerpiece, more like a religious object on an altar than a pretty toy on a dresser top.

Celeste looked over her limited wardrobe and chose a dress covered with glittering sequins to wear to dinner. She watched her shimmering silver image in the mirror, while the maid, a fat peasant woman with a coil of black braids atop her head, stared amazed. She had never in her life seen such beauty.

There was a knock at the door. Dron was back, ready to take her where she did not want to go, to the dining room for a formal introduction to the émigrés. She wandered again through the twisting corridors of this palatial manor house now deserted except for an occasional servant dozing in a chair or standing at attention. Dron led her past the huge dining hall, where formal banquets were given, and opened the door to the smaller, more informal dining room. As Celeste entered, all conversation stopped.

Seated around the table were thirty caricatures out of a novel of Russian upper-class life. A few smiled grudgingly, but most just stared at her. She was an intruder pushing her way into their closed little world.

At one end of the table sat the countess, presiding over them all. "This is Celeste Dorchester," she announced.

The émigrés nodded and were introduced one by one, all by their old titles. After the introductions they ignored Celeste. Talk went around Celeste in great circles.

"They go on and on about people who died a decade ago," she thought. "They're all so threadbare and seem so tired. No wonder the young stay away. Why, this house is nothing but a great tomb, a house of death."

Then the door opened, and another émigré arrived, a woman. She was younger than the others, about forty, and she was different. She was as modern as jazz.

The countess said, "Princess Xenia, I've warned you before not to be late to dinner."

"Sorry," the woman answered smoothly, "but I couldn't help it." She made her way to her place, then looked curiously at Celeste.

On the face of it this was the one person in the room Celeste might have anything in common with, so she tried to smile and found she couldn't. She didn't like Princess Xenia. The woman was all too familiar, a café society type straight from the nightclubs of Paris and the gaming tables of Monte Carlo. At sight of her Celeste looked away and listened to the émigrés.

"Why, the clothes of 1910 can't compare to the clothes of the nineties, Madame Scherova."

"My dear Madame Vladimira, what are you saying?"

"That the nineties were an especially elegant decade, that's all. My mother had the most beautiful dresses then. She kept the peasant girls busy sewing pearls on her gowns. It took them months. They went blind from the sewing."

Went blind! Celeste shivered at this glimpse of the dark side of Old Russia.

From the other end of the table an old man cried, "I don't care if Gregory Romanov was the czar's cousin. He knew nothing about dogs. I kept the finest kennels in Russia."

"True, true," cried a bald, dwarfish man, still wearing the military decorations he'd won in the czarist army. "I always said, 'Go to Prince Stolypin if you want a good borzoi.' "

"You understand hunting, Your Excellency."

"I never liked it, Prince. Give me army life. Since Peter the Great we have had a general in every generation of my family."

Amused, Princess Xenia tried to catch Celeste's eye. "See what fools the other émigrés are," she seemed to be saying.

Celeste did not so much as glance at her.

"Did you hear about Sergei?" cried a little woman bright as a bird. "He's dead. The gas stove. Creditors, I believe." She snickered. "He was so arrogant when he owned three estates and four hundred souls."

The countess called for silence. "It is time for a toast," she said.

Prohibition was the law in America, but that meant nothing to the countess. Her wine cellars were full.

"To the czar!" someone cried.

"To the czar!" they all echoed. Except for Princess Xenia. She continued to eat.

They went down the list of Romanovs, alive and dead, straight to the Dowager Empress Marie Feodorovna, still living in Denmark.

And for a moment, despite their strangeness, Celeste felt compassion for them. Who knew better than she how awful it was to lose a whole world?

Celeste saw in her mind's eye the gold wall sconces that used to line the corridors of grand hotels and gave the air a pink electric glow when the lights were turned on. She saw the spacious rooms in the hotels, the long mirrors, the french doors leading out to balconies overlooking the sea. She saw servants, legions of them, smoothing life's every detail, ordering a cab when one was needed, serving coffee and sweets on silver trays. As unhappy as her childhood had been, going from wealth to poverty had been terrible.

Except for the countess' generosity the émigrés had nothing. Neither did Princess Xenia. She had a hungry look.

"Miss Dorchester?" Princess Xenia called out to her.

"Yes."

The entire room fell silent.

"I understand you're a Fabergé collector."

"At this point I'm just beginning. I hope someday to be an important dealer, but it will take time."

"How will you manage till then?"

"When I've learned enough, I'll go back to Paris."

Princess Xenia sighed. "Lucky woman," she said.

"I'll have to begin by working for someone else, of course, on commission. Buy what I can for myself at the best bargains I can find as I go along. Eventually I'll strike out on my own. Set up my own shop."

"How efficient you sound," said Princess Xenia a little sarcastically.

"I have no idea if I'm efficient or not," said Celeste. "I've never worked."

"Celeste's father was efficient, a very fine businessman," said the countess.

"Oh, yes, the notorious Nigel Dorchester, who made all our Russian ladies swoon in the good old days."

"Xenia, why are you always rude?" The countess shook her head. "If it weren't for Anatole, I'd have nothing to do with you."

"My husband, Anatole, is a hero, Celeste," said Xenia. "He was wounded fighting against the Bolsheviks. He lives, but he doesn't live. You see, he's totally paralyzed. I pay an old couple in Provence to take care of him."

Overcome, Celeste made some banal remark.

"And she won't let me help," complained the countess. "I would give him anything."

"Anatole is mine," Princess Xenia said proudly. "My responsibility, not yours."

"I could fix everything with one word to Boris Berg. He has a list of my personal causes."

Xenia didn't respond to the countess.

"Boris Berg," one of the émigrés complained. "That petit bourgeois prig. He has no use for us, Countess, no use for any of us."

"Who is Boris Berg?" Celeste asked.

The countess answered, "In Russia I would have called him my steward. You will be seeing him soon, Celeste. In fact, you'll be seeing a great deal of him."

"How boring for you," Xenia said. "Still, he's right about us all, you know. We are parasites, those of us who aren't laboring like serfs, making our livings driving cabs in Paris and running restaurants."

"Parasites!" There was an uproar at the table.

To calm them, to prevent a quarrel, Madame Vladimire cried, "Oh, do let's have one more toast. To our dear patroness, Countess Ustinova."

It worked. The émigrés were diverted. They raised their glasses in a dramatic toast, then sent them crashing against the fireplace.

"Oh, my precious friends," said the countess with quiet dignity, "your toast means a great deal to me."

Just as she spoke, a man stepped into the room.

Celeste's throat went dry.

"Ah, Nicholas," the countess cried, "you are back early. Well, my dear boy, you have been missed."

Princess Xenia said, "Yes, indeed. Really missed, *chéri*." And she made *chéri* sound as inviting as a kiss.

But the man did not look at Xenia. He did not look at the countess either. He had eyes only for Celeste.

"Nicholas. I want you to meet Celeste Dorchester," said the countess.

"We've met," the man said.

"You've met?"

"Yes, quite by accident," said Celeste, trying to sound casual. "In Paris, at an exhibition. We fell in love." Pointedly, she added, "With the Azov Diamond."

Chapter V

She was here! Nicholas couldn't believe it. He was a man of the world and so exercised perfect self-control, but as he went around the table greeting the émigrés, he thought he was dreaming.

The countess had told him before he left that a girl named Celeste Dorchester was coming to stay, but what had that meant? The girl was merely an abstraction, a detail. What a surprise to discover that she was the woman he'd met in Paris!

That encounter had left him so restless and preoccupied he'd returned early. Did she guess? Had she any idea at all about the danger at Nov, the intrigue?

He sat down next to the countess, who fawned over him as if he were a favorite child.

"He's cool, I'll give him that much," Celeste thought.

Nicholas looked at her. She averted her eyes.

"Oh, you pirate," she thought. "Life with you would be a whirlwind of excitement, of passionate ups and deplorable downs. I won't put up with those downs, I won't." But it took all her steadying reason to keep her eyes off him.

Then the countess said, "So you already know my dear Nicholas Bazdeev."

Bazdeev? Why, he was no more a Bazdeev than she was. What was he doing here? What did he want? He wasn't Russian. She'd guessed he was an American that day they'd met in Paris, and he hadn't contradicted her.

"How was Paris?" Xenia asked him.

He answered, "Interesting."

"Something must have spoiled your trip, *chéri,* or you wouldn't have come back early."

"The trip went stale."

Xenia gave Celeste a calculating glance.

"I'm glad it did," said Countess Ustinova. "I haven't enjoyed being without my chauffeur. Even though you've only been with me three months, Nicholas, I've gotten quite used to you."

Three months and already off for a little trip to Paris? My, my, wasn't the countess tolerant!

"Nicholas' father was a great landowner in Russia, Celeste. We émigrés thought he'd died during the Revolution. We were wrong. Nicholas and his father escaped and reached America."

"The journey was too much for my father," Nicholas said smoothly. "It killed him. Luckily I was only nineteen and very strong."

"Liar," Celeste thought, stabbing away at her food, while she condemned the countess for being gullible.

"He went his own way. Didn't get in touch with any of us. Can you imagine such a thing?"

"Dear Countess, at that time I wanted to cut my ties with the past. I intended to become fully American."

"You knew me," Princess Xenia said. "Consider what you owe me, Helene, for having brought him here. You need some young blood at Nov."

"Ah, how sad that the son of my old friend Alexis Bazdeev should be down on his luck and in need of work. To think of the balls and parties your father gave in Moscow."

"True, Countess," said Nicholas. "Of course, it's been years, and I've forgotten so many things. Still, it seems to me the parties you give here at Nov are quite as pleasant."

"There are traditions we must not let die."

"I'm happy to do my part in keeping them alive," said Nicholas, savoring the wine and caviar.

"I hate him," Celeste thought. "Look at him, living off

the poor countess. He's almost as bad as the gigolos who used to take money from my mother. He's detestable."

Abruptly Celeste stood up. The silver dress sparkled. Against the sequins, like drops of ice, her skin had the look of alabaster warmed by the sun.

She made excuses, said she was tired, and left. In the hall she found Dron, and docilely she let him lead her back to her room. The maid was still waiting. She let the woman help her undress, then dismissed her. She put the silver dress on again and cautiously opened the door.

Something was going on in this house, something wrong. Nicholas' presence pointed to that. He wasn't here just to take treats from the countess.

There was no sign of the maid or, thankfully, of Dron. For a second she hesitated. She wouldn't want to be discovered wandering aimlessly about the house. She thought again of the crying girl. How did she fit in? And even if she found the girl, Madame Kropotkina was probably still with her. But the sound of the girl's weeping haunted Celeste.

She made her way by ducking into doorways to avoid servants. Only one, a liveried footman, an anachronism from the days of coaches, caught sight of her. He stared at her suspiciously, but once he was gone she ran. She stopped, baffled.

"This is the right corridor, I'm sure of it," she thought. "But where is the malachite vase? They must have moved it so I wouldn't find this corridor again."

She walked slowly, pausing before each door, uncertain what to do. Then like the rush of the wind came the terrified whisper: "Help me. Oh, please help me before it's too late."

She whirled around. Silence.

"Tell me what's going on," Celeste said softly. "I promise I will try to help."

There wasn't a sound. Perplexed, Celeste tried desperately to think of what to do.

Somewhere in this enormous house there must be someone she could turn to. They couldn't all be dangerous, could they? There must be one decent human being in the lot.

Feeling oddly like Diogenes bearing his lantern through Athens in search of one honest man, she went downstairs and hurried to the main part of the house. Then she heard the rustle of papers coming from a room on her left. The room drew her like a magnet. Its door was open. She could see inside. At a huge pigeonhole desk a man sat working, his face studious as he scratched away with a pen. A pool of lamplight illuminated him.

He looked clumsy, but perhaps that was because he was too big even for that big desk. He wasn't handsome. The clothes he wore were poorly cut, and he had very unglamorous spectacles. He reminded Celeste of a great Russian bear.

He noticed her and rose.

She looked into his eyes. They were very blue and wonderfully kind.

Then he smiled. It was a smile that came straight from the soul. She had seen pictures of men like him, writers and intellectuals in Old Russia, members of the intelligentsia, they were called. He wasn't worldly and cosmopolitan like the other émigrés. He wouldn't speak French effortlessly or prefer Paris to Moscow.

No, Russia was in his bloodstream. Other than Dron, he was the only authentic Russian in this house.

Celeste had no doubt who he was.

"Boris Berg," she said. "They mentioned you at dinner tonight."

"You must be Celeste Dorchester." He came up to her, took her hand in greeting. Her hand was lost in his. He towered over her. She had to look up at him as if she were a child.

"We will be working together," he said. "I am in charge of the countess' jewels, and that includes her Fabergé collection. I will do my best to teach you as much as I can."

Celeste trusted him. He was her honest man; she took

the plunge. "There's a girl hidden away here. I don't know why. Please help me rescue her."

Boris's face lost its kindness. He became severe.

"There's one lesson you'd better learn quickly. Ask no questions. Do not interfere. That is the only way you can survive at Nov."

Chapter VI

Celeste was horrified. He was cautious and selfish, not at all heroic. Her disappointment showed.

"But the girl's in terrible trouble."

"It is no business of yours," he said emphatically.

"So you know about her?"

He didn't answer.

"Yet you do nothing to free her?"

Celeste watched him closely. Then it hit her. "You're very loyal to the countess, aren't you?"

She saw by the look on his face that he was.

"So you are a man of honor. You won't talk about this girl because Countess Ustinova told you not to. Why are you so loyal?" she asked boldly.

"I owe her everything. I didn't get out of Russia until 1921, and things went very hard for me. I don't know if you can understand what it means to be a Russian living in exile. A German calls his native country the fatherland. You Americans have your Uncle Sam. But to us, Russia is the motherland. We love her as if we were her children, and we are never happy away from her."

"You still miss your home as deeply as that?"

"Every day of my life," Boris said so passionately that Celeste was awed. "Of course, I can bear my suffering more easily here at Nov because the countess has so carefully planted a Russian village, nurtured it, and made it grow."

"So that's why you stay."

"That and because I believe in doing my duty."

"How long have you been here?"

"Three years."

"May I speak freely?" Celeste asked.

Stiffly he answered, "I do not carry tales. Say what you like."

"My father considered the countess a mad schemer. One year she ordered her peasants to migrate north to await the Second Coming. Then she changed her mind and set them to growing plants she thought had magical healing powers. Every peasant walking to Petersburg to try to see the czar stopped to see her. Every village priest who claimed to have witnessed a miracle spoke with her. She shared their messianic delusions. Good thing she had Count Ustinov to restrain her."

"In my own way," he said quietly, "I have helped restrain her, too."

"I see. From affection or duty?"

"Why do you ask?"

"Duty is such an austere concept."

"Is it?" He smiled again, so gloriously that she felt quite captured by him. "I have always worked hard. But then I have always been strong. When I was taken prisoner, it was my strength that helped me survive."

"So you were a soldier."

"I fought with the White Army of the czar during the Civil War. The Bolsheviks would have killed me, but I escaped. I roamed the taiga alone in the winter. I survived by hunting and by drinking enough vodka to keep warm. Occasionally I ran into trappers, peasants who were loyal. They helped me. When I crossed the border, I did any kind of work. I have many skills, but I couldn't settle down. I kept hoping the Bolsheviks would be defeated so I could go home. But they won."

Celeste was deeply moved. Softly she asked, "Where is your home?"

"Smolensk. It is a very old city, and it's seen its share of war and destruction. My father was a schoolmaster there."

"Where is your father?"

"He was killed by soldiers. My mother, too. She was beaten to death."

"Oh, no."

Boris was not looking at her. He was seeing violent and terrible scenes. Celeste thought about her own rather pointless life and felt very shallow.

"The countess' guests are not the whole story of Old Russia," Boris said. "Had they been, I myself would have become a Bolshevik. I despised the nobility when I was a child, and I despise them now. The countess' guests are stupid and frivolous."

It occurred to Celeste how she must look in her silver dress. Frivolous.

"You don't approve of frivolity," she said.

He answered with a simple unqualified no. And she sensed that although she'd been dazzled by him he was hardly overwhelmed by her. It was a new sensation for Celeste. She'd been a beauty since the cradle.

"But there were others," Boris went on. "People like my parents who were deeply religious. Peasants who cultivated the land and who felt a deep mystical bond with the czar. Fresh young girls in villages who—"

He stopped, but Celeste was shaken. "Yes?" she asked.

"Never mind," he said. She wondered if it wasn't out of kindness so as not to point out how different they were from modern girls in silver dresses cut too low.

Celeste thought of rose-cheeked peasant girls with dark eyes, their hair hidden under brilliantly colored kerchiefs. She felt like crying.

"Won't you leave here someday?" she asked, meaning, "Won't you ever forget the past?"

"Unless it's to return to Moscow, no. And so you won't think she's taking advantage of me, I must tell you the countess pays me very well. My savings grow by the day."

"What are you saving for?"

It was an impertinent question. He didn't answer.

"Well, I'm not going to stay here forever," Celeste cried. "Not me. Nov's a frightening place. And as for your precious countess, do you know she's set a servant to watching me? I'm going to Paris and enjoy its glitter as soon as I can. I can't wait until I'm a rich Fabergé dealer."

"If that is what you want, then I hope life gives it to you. I hope you will become as important as Henry Winters."

"Henry Winters? Why, he's one of the leading jewel dealers in the world. I'll never be his equal."

"Who knows? Perhaps the countess will abandon him and take you up, make you her dealer in his place."

"I can't imagine such a thing. Why, when I was in New York, I went to Fifth Avenue just to look into Henry Winters' store window. It's a marvelous place, better even than the brightest jewelry stores in Paris. It's in one of those towering New York skyscrapers. I never saw finer silver and china or such porcelain and gold."

"We wouldn't know here at Nov. The countess doesn't travel. All jewels are personally brought here for her inspection by Henry Winters himself."

"Oh, what's he like?"

"A very pleasant old man who knows how to defer to a rich clientele."

"I remember when my father received such treatment," Celeste said. "He'd snap his fingers and gems would appear." She sighed.

"I take it he had more difficulty acquiring the Easter egg," Boris said dryly.

"You know about my egg?"

"Of course. The countess told me you have it."

"My father was not a very honorable man, I'm afraid. He came across the egg on a back street in Paris in a seedy little shop run by a Greek antique dealer named Condopolous. My father claimed that Condopolous had no idea the egg was an authentic Fabergé and sold it cheap."

"And you don't believe that story."

"Not in the least."

Boris returned to his desk. "You are too critical of your father. Even dealers can be ruthless when it comes to fine jewels. The countess never asks Henry Winters where he gets his gemstones. Now, if you don't mind, I must return to my work."

"You really are dedicated to duty."

"Promise me one thing before you go," Boris said.

"What's that?"

"You won't bother anymore about the girl. You'll ignore her, pretend she doesn't exist."

"Why should I make such a promise to you?"

"Trust me. It's good advice."

Celeste hesitated, looked closely at his gentle face, then said, "All right, I will trust you. I won't try to find her again. But please tell me about that woman Madame Kropotkina, who guards the girl. Oh, don't pretend she doesn't. I've seen her."

"That woman is a total abomination," Boris said with stunning emotion. "Evil and decadent. But there, I will not gossip. If you want to learn her story, ask anyone. There are plenty who will tell you."

"But if she's so terrible, why is she tolerated? Why does the countess let her stay at Nov?"

"Because," Boris said ominously, "Madame Kropotkina is the countess' sister."

"What?"

"It's true. So Madame Kropotkina comes and goes as she pleases." He added, "No matter what she does."

Chapter VII

"Exactly what has Madame Kropotkina done?" Celeste asked Princess Xenia.

Celeste had been as good as her word. For two weeks she'd kept away from the corridor where she'd heard that desperate cry for help, even though her conscience bothered her.

Besides, she hadn't been completely free to visit it again. Dron was spying on her. He didn't dog her footsteps, nothing so obvious now. But she'd often come across him peering at her as she rounded a corner or waiting for her when she arrived in a room. And at least one night she was sure that he'd posted himself outside her room. He was watching her closely all right.

"Acting on the countess' orders," Celeste had said to herself irately.

"So you've come to me," Xenia said.

Celeste said, "There was no one else. The other émigrés shut me out. They evade my questions."

Xenia wore a robe of bright, splashy colors as if to combat winter, for the snow covered the prairie now and the lake was ice. She looked like a tropical flower picked out of season.

"Why should I tell you anything? You've been very unpleasant." Hatred cracked in Xenia's voice.

Celeste knew she'd made a bad enemy. But even as she looked at Xenia's raised penciled eyebrows and the over-painted face, she couldn't hide her disgust.

"You," Xenia spit, "have a lot of nerve looking down at me. How dare you feel such contempt? You're young and beautiful, and you think that counts for everything. But I was once both those things and more. I was one of the richest women in Moscow. Spent my winters in the Crimea, my summers under the Mediterranean sun. Perhaps you're jealous of me over Nicholas."

Oh, the stupid woman. Didn't Xenia know that Nicholas maneuvered himself into being alone with Celeste every chance he got? Didn't she see how disloyal he was, ready to betray any woman as soon as another, prettier one came along?

"I don't care about Nicholas."

"Oh, yes, you do," Xenia said. "I know the signs. Your heart beats a little bit faster every time he's around."

Celeste bit her lip so as not to hurl at Xenia the words "You're wrong. I'm falling in love with Boris Berg."

She spent hours with Boris every day poring over Fabergé's little treasures. In three years the countess had done much to educate him.

"You're so transparent," sneered Xenia. "You're standing there now telling yourself you love Boris Berg. But you love him only with your head. Your heart craves Nicholas. He has your emotions. Without emotion there is no love. But you're very smug about what you feel toward Boris. You think I'm incapable of such a fine spiritual love."

Celeste saw Xenia as she'd look entering the casino at Monte Carlo, wearing last year's furs and rhinestones she hoped would pass muster, keeping her eye out for a man with money. It wasn't a pleasant picture.

"I love Anatole as you could never dream of loving Boris. We were the perfect fairy-tale couple. When we were married, my father had the peasants throw bushels of violets along the road. The wheels of our coach crushed them and made the air fragrant and sweet. Now Anatole is nothing but a crushed object."

"How terrible!" Celeste said, and for a moment she pitied Xenia.

"Do you know what I have to contend with, Celeste? The old couple who care for Anatole have their hands out for money all the time. I must live as I can. So you have no right to feel superior to me. It's a shame we can't be friends. I don't like Nov either. It's the jazz age, it's the twenties. I want to Charleston. At Nov they waltz."

"You don't have to stay," Celeste said.

"No?" Xenia was bitter. "What does one do when one's broke? Well, look at you. Better to be here where Countess Ustinova provides banquets and balls, baccarat and Gypsies for our amusement. Oh, yes, Gypsies who once lived on the countess' estates come every winter. I admit I'm a beggar. But so are you. I resent it. Almost as much as Madame K."

"Madame Kropotkina?"

Xenia's eye were slits. "The countess hasn't treated her very well over the years. Oh, she puts up with her nowadays. They're both growing older. But Natalia can never be sure when the countess' generosity will run dry."

"What's she like?" Celeste cried earnestly. "Tell me what she's like."

"Natalia?" Xenia was thoughtful. "She was the scandal of Old Russia, a black sheep. Ran off with the countess' lover. No, not her husband. The boy Helene was engaged to before she met the count. Natalia was already married at the time to old General Kropotkin. Married him because he was very rich. But she couldn't stick it. She took off for the border. Eventually she abandoned her sister's fiancé and went through a whole string of lovers. For years Helene would have nothing to do with her. She made her way through Egypt and the Orient as a cheap spiritualist. She survived. Oh, she's a wily old devil."

Celeste was puzzled. "But I don't understand."

"What?"

"I'd had the impression she'd done something awful. Evil."

Princess Xenia moved closer. She lowered her voice. "The day she ran away from old Kropotkin, her husband, servants found him dead in a chair. He'd been stabbed to death. One of the servants was hanged for it, but everyone whispered that the real murderer was Natalia. It's all gossip, of course."

Was it? Celeste was horrified. "Help me," that poor girl had cried. "Help me, please." And Boris wouldn't help. Celeste couldn't bear it. She needed to find Boris, to reassure herself about him.

She hurried away. Every window she passed showed a bleak scene, for it was snowing again. "Winter," Celeste thought, "the Russian season." She had the fantasy that somehow Nov had actually been moved to Russia in the night. She felt desolate. Had she wandered into a strange nomadic camp where murderers were tolerated? Murderers and what else? she wondered.

She walked past a huge tiled stove, the sort which heated every part of the house and made it oppressively, almost deliriously warm. A glance into the cardroom showed the émigrés losing handfuls of pennies as they'd once lost rubles by the thousands. A servant waited on them. He wore the vest, balloon trousers, and fez of a court blackamoor, and he gave each émigré an orchid in defiance of winter. An old peasant woman, bowed and submissive, a kerchief on her head, was pouring a glass of tea for Madame Vladimira from a silver samovar. It was a scene from another time.

Celeste found Boris in the study, Fabergé toys spilled across his desk like so much jeweled litter. He was examining the statuette of a peasant, a sly little kulak made of tourmaline.

She watched his hands. They were gentle, so gentle, yet she knew Boris was as strong as a blade of steel. Inwardly, too, he was powerful. Of course, she could trust him. He was everything she thought he was. He must have a reason for not helping that girl. But what could it be? She wanted to curl up in his strength, to make it part of herself.

Then he looked at Celeste, and her heart dropped. How ironic that she had found at last the man she wanted only to discover that he was thoroughly indifferent to her.

"What's wrong?" he asked with avuncular interest.

"Nothing," she lied. She'd promised to trust him, and she would.

"Shall we begin then?" he asked. "Yesterday we were speaking of jadeite," he went on didactically. "Shall we continue examining its properties?"

She sighed.

He became concerned. "Am I overworking you?"

"You're a hard taskmaster. My head's been stuffed with facts."

"It's only a beginning. It takes years to become an expert. I am not yet really one myself. For that you must turn to a man from the upper classes, like Nicholas Bazdeev. His knowledge of jewels is astounding. He can tell you all about Fabergé. He can identify all the hallmarks; that's important, you know, in identifying frauds. You'll need that kind of information. Perhaps you should speak to him."

"Spare me that," Celeste murmured.

"Once I discussed Fabergé's Finnish craftsmen with Nicholas. He had a wealth of detail on them. Quite extraordinary when you consider that Fabergé had them overseeing seven hundred workers in his factories. As for Fabergé himself, Nicholas knows everything. Yes, I do believe, Celeste, he really is your man."

Celeste seethed. This was hardly what she wanted to hear.

"Sometimes I think you'd be happiest as a monk," she said, miserably.

Boris stared at her in confusion. "I am not an ascetic," he said, and got up. He turned his back on her and faced the broad window behind his desk.

Wasn't he? She'd read about Russian mystics who'd abandoned the world.

"Look," he said, staring at something outside, and she was startled by the joy he showed. "It is a scene from my childhood. The peasants have taken out sleighs."

She joined him and watched the horses moving smoothly through the snow. The wind whipped the edges of the blankets which covered the peasants in their wooden sleighs and kept them warm.

Boris pointed toward the lake, where the peasants were skating. Then he opened the window a little. The prairie cold rushed in. He cried, "Listen!"

They were singing as only Russians can. "The folk songs of the motherland," Boris said, deeply moved. "The sight takes me back." There was such mourning in his voice that Celeste touched him gently in sympathy for the barest second.

But Boris was like stone.

When he turned back to her, he was all business. "We needn't spend any more time on Fabergé just now."

He went to the safe on the study wall, opened it, and took out velvet-lined trays, on which diamonds shone like stars, and little drawstring bags, each containing a jewel. Celeste felt a passionate desire akin to hunger for them all. She remembered a folktale she'd heard in Russia about a princess who was served gems instead of food. Celeste could fancy herself at such a feast, her plate piled high with lovely pearls and merry topazes.

But these weren't topazes. Boris was showing her magnificent jewels. She glowed with life at the sight of them, but Boris was indifferent.

"You think I have no soul," he said, "because they don't excite me."

"No, I think you have a Russian soul. You live for the spirit. To you these are nothing but dead minerals."

He put the jewels back. "I make a point of remaining detached from things."

"But you aren't immune to everything. Look how you enjoy the sleighs and the skaters," Celeste thought. And considered sadly to herself, "Yet you are detached in some ways. You're completely unmoved by me."

Chapter VIII

"How dark it is tonight," Celeste thought, staring out of the window of her room. "No moon, no stars, and the wind so loud."

Celeste still hadn't got used to the winter wind on the prairie, where it howls, unchallenged, like a great wolf. Celeste bent her head over her book and again tried to read. It was a great tome on Fabergé which Boris had given her.

When she heard the knock on the door, she was curious and wary. Who was it at this hour of the night?

She opened the door.

"Dron!" she said, startled. "What do you want?"

He looked around the room, probing, taking in everything.

"Well?"

He mumbled in Russian and handed her a note.

"Do you really know so little English, I wonder?" Celeste asked.

He stared at her blankly, and she slammed the door in his face.

The note was from the countess. "I am lonely for my dear dead czarevich. Would you bring your Easter egg to my sitting room? I want to look upon the dear child's face again, and I have never seen a better likeness than your little portrait."

She took the egg and left her room. Dron was gone, but she knew he would reappear if she didn't go straight to the countess. As she walked, she listened to the wind.

"It roars as if a whole battle of soldiers were fighting in the sky," she thought.

The fighting grew louder, raged on, became fierce. She realized it wasn't the wind now. There was a terrible quarrel going on. Of all places, in the countess' sitting room. Celeste waited outside.

"I won't be treated like a charity case, Helene."

"Lower your voice, Xenia."

"Why should I?"

"Because shouting's for shrews and fishwives."

"Then leave me alone. Stop telling me how I should behave. I'll do as I please."

"How dare you!"

"I dare anything I like; you know that."

"All too well. Your reputation's in tatters. You're a disgrace."

"I'm sick of your insults. I can't live a life of celibacy."

"But must you live on what you take from men? A princess of the Russian court does not sell herself."

"I require bright lights and champagne, not ghosts of the past."

"Think of Anatole."

Xenia's voice merged with the wind. "I do think of him. Constantly. But he'll never be better. When I visit him, I always find him lying in bed in the same twisted way, staring at the ceiling."

"None of that excuses what you do. Shameful, shameful."

"Know what really upsets you, Helene? That I have Nicholas. He reminds you of that lover your sister stole from you. Madame K. says Nicholas looks like him. Well, at least you can't say I'm attracted to Nicholas for his money."

"Don't be absurd. I adore Nicholas, of course, but as if he were a son. I've taken enough from you, Xenia, for one night. Now get out."

"All right, but I'll get even with you."

"Yes, yes, I know. You're going to be rich, dancing in gold. You'll go to Paris again. Show me up. Well, I'm expecting Celeste Dorchester, so please nurse your dreams of independence and revenge somewhere else."

There was a pause. Then very softly Xenia said, "You have dreams, too, don't you, Helene? Quite glorious ones. Watch out I don't ruin them for you."

The door flew open, and Xenia rushed out, looking as if the Furies were at her. She raged past Celeste blindly.

"Come in, come in," Countess Ustinova called to Celeste. The countess looked utterly distracted.

"Xenia couldn't mean it," the countess said. "No, I won't believe it of her, a daughter of Old Russia. I wouldn't believe it of any of them."

"Believe what?" Celeste asked sharply.

The countess turned her confused stare on Celeste. "Never mind," she said, shaking her head. "I'm being foolish." She made an effort to regain her dignity. "We Russians can be highly volatile people. Now let me see your egg."

The countess took it, held it up as if it were a drug she'd been seeking. She opened all the little doors and gazed at the tiny portraits. "See them? What an artist Fabergé was."

"I know," said Celeste. "I look at the portraits often and admire them."

The countess relaxed as she looked at the egg. Her eyes had a dreamy glow as if her mind were again taking her into the past. "What celebrations we had in the old days! In the Russian Orthodox Church there is no holiday as wonderful as Easter. Can you see it, Celeste, as I see it? My sleigh carries me to the bright churches. I toss silver coins to the beggars in the snow."

The countess went on. Vaguely at first; then, with growing freshness, Celeste did recall the Russian Easter. She remembered standing in the center of a crowded square in Moscow, holding a candle. Before her was a huge church so filled with people she and her father couldn't get in. The church was bright with the soft golden flames of a thousand candles. Suddenly crowds flowed from the church. Her father held her up so she could see. The candlelight looked like a broad Russian river of fire. Then the river flowed as everyone walked around the church, led by the priest, and returned to find Christ had risen.

"Because of the climate, the coming of spring in Russia is magic, Celeste. That is why we love our Easters so. Though we always managed to survive the winter well enough. New Year's was the start of our season. I'll never forget the opening of the ballet, the Gypsies coming to the palace to tell our fortunes. Ask Boris Berg about them sometime. He understands their customs. He's a true Slavophile."

"Boris knows about many things," said Celeste, and thought to herself, "and nothing at all about love." Then she remembered the way he had talked about the fresh peasant girls of Russia, and she felt weak and frightened. Somewhere in his life there had to be a woman. What if there was someone Boris still loved? Firmly Celeste pushed the idea away, closed her mind to it.

"We danced until dawn at Grand Duke Gregory's winter balls," the countess said, still spinning dreams. "How we feasted! And he always gave us special treats, trinkets made by Fabergé."

"Fabergé, always Fabergé," mused Celeste.

"Well, there was no one like him in Europe. Entering his Petersburg shop was, well, I can only describe it as a sobering experience. No place was more solid and secure. One felt that one was in a bank. There was not a sound to be heard, and on either side of the shop were long glass cases. I'd be surprised if Henry Winters' can compare to it. In the cases were perfect toys: tiny animals with jeweled eyes and enameled flowers in silver baskets."

"And now so many of them are here."

"Many, but not all."

"They're marvelous."

"Expressions of an age, an age with time for leisure and beauty." The countess changed. She burned with an inner fire and held the egg so tightly Celeste was afraid she'd damage it.

"The Bolsheviks killed the spirit of that age," the countess said violently, "just as they destroyed Fabergé himself. Oh, they didn't murder him with bullets, but he was an old man, and when they forced him into exile, he died. Then do you know what they did, those brutes, those barbarians? They made Fabergé's son fix a price to all of Russia's great gemstones. He sat in a room with our most splendid jewels heaped in a pile and sorted them, while one of their fanatics kept watch over him. They say Madame Oupenskaya's pearls were among them. They were one of the best strands in the world, a gift from Grand Duke Gregory to her when she was one of the great ballerinas of Russia." The countess' eyes flashed with hatred. "We'll never know, of course, if they were really there. They seem to have vanished from the world. The Bolsheviks sold so many jewels. They said they needed the money to establish a worker's paradise. Claimed they had to build factories and schools. Russia's pride, her glory, sold to foreigners. Horrible, horrible."

She began to babble so wildly about Bolsheviks and murderers that Celeste, horrified, yet fascinated, got away as soon as she could. She took one last glance at the countess through the open door.

Countess Ustinova was still talking.

"I'll get Boris," Celeste thought. "Perhaps he can calm her. Does she even realize she's alone?"

"Boris!" Celeste called as she burst into the study where she knew Boris generally stayed, working until the wee hours of the morning. "Come quickly. It's the countess." Her words died.

Boris wasn't there. But Nicholas was. The door of the wall safe stood open with Nicholas beside it, a tray of diamonds in his hand.

"So you are a jewel thief! What happened to the real Nicholas Bazdeev? Did the Russians murder him a decade ago, or did you dispose of him yourself?"

As soon as the words were out of her mouth, she regretted them, for with the jewels Nicholas held glittering like baubles from a treasure chest, he looked more piratical than ever.

"Better watch what you say, Celeste." He put down the tray, came up to her. She huddled against the wall in fear. "I don't like your accusations. You could get hurt saying things like that."

"I promise I won't tell the countess I found you here. And I won't say a word about your being an American." She let out a cry of pain. He was gripping her arm tightly, so tightly that she felt it going numb.

"Please," she whispered in terror.

"You're right, Celeste. You're not going to say a word to the countess. If she believes what you say, then I'm in trouble. And if she doesn't believe you, then you're in trouble. Neither of us wants that."

He let go of her arm. It was bruised.

"You fascinate me, Celeste. You have ever since Paris. But don't press your luck. I'm not mild-mannered like your Boris Berg. I have no intention of letting you ruin things for me by getting me packed off to jail."

He looked down at her, studied her face closely, as if to read her thoughts. "Damn, you're thinking of Boris, aren't you? Hoping he'll come and rescue you."

"No." She shook her head.

"Don't lie to me. Why do you want him? You have such flair."

"Too much. I don't need daily convulsions, emotional trauma."

"You don't need someone plodding and boring, a sanctimonious prig like Boris. I'm tired of the way you catch his every word as if it were a jewel. I could tell you something about him you wouldn't want to hear."

"What?" she asked. Then she cried desperately, "No, don't tell me. I don't want to hear."

"Then learn to see him straight. He works from morning till night like the meanest serf. He doesn't know how life can sparkle. He's a barbarian."

She found the courage to defend Boris. "You don't understand him, so you can't appreciate him. He's disciplined; he has principles. He's brilliant, too. He's read all the great Russian writers, Tolstoy, Gogol. You should hear him describe his escape from Russia."

"You're making a fool out of yourself. Wearing your heart on your sleeve." Nicholas sounded furious.

To Celeste's horror he flicked the light switch off.

"I had hoped you'd want me."

"A jewel thief? Never."

"Why not? Jewel thieves lead lives of high adventure."

Nicholas put his mouth over Celeste's and kissed her with such competence that for a moment she lost track of everything. Her Dorchester instincts triumphed.

Then she remembered the bruise on her arm, and her strongest sensation was fear. She managed to pull free and turn the light on.

"I could strangle you for your stupidity," Nicholas said. He brought her hands up to her throat. "You and I could be golden people, dancing through what's left of the decade if you'd stop fighting your true feelings."

"I love Boris."

He let her go, reached into his pocket, and brought out a sparkling diamond.

"Put it back. Don't rob the countess."

"Here." He dropped it into Celeste's hand.

"What?"

"Take it to her." He laughed. "That's why I came here tonight. The countess is in a sentimental mood. This morning she asked me to go to her safe when I had the time and bring her one of her precious jewels. This diamond belonged to a girl who was murdered in a serf uprising in 1917. The girl was flogged to death. Do you think the countess will enjoy reminiscing over that?"

Celeste dropped the diamond as if it were a hot coal, turned, and ran, while Nicholas stood where he was, still laughing.

She ran for all she was worth right back to her room, and she started to open the door. A hand grabbed hers and pulled her inside. The room was dark, and for one eerie and terrifying minute she thought she was facing

Nicholas again. But that was absurd. He couldn't have reached her room before she had.

"Hush," a voice whispered. "Please don't scream. I've come to you for help."

Celeste felt her pulse race. She knew immediately who it was—the weeping girl.

The light came on.

Celeste almost collapsed. She looked into the wide-set eyes, stared at the expressive mouth of the woman before her. The face was older, of course, but totally recognizable.

She had seen the face before, a dozen times, a hundred times, gazing at her from behind one of the pearl-handled doors set into the Easter egg. There was no question whose face it was.

Celeste was looking straight at the Grand Duchess Tatiana Romanova, second daughter of Alexandra and Nicholas II, deceased emperor and autocrat of all the Russias.

"But you're dead, too," she whispered inanely. "All the czar's family is dead."

Chapter IX

"You're looking at me very skeptically," the girl said. "You don't believe me."

"Frankly, no."

"It's doubt like yours that's kept me alive all these years."

Celeste studied the girl's face, then caught herself. This wasn't a girl; this was a woman, easily thirty years old, exactly the age the Grand Duchess Tatiana would be.

"Why then does she seem to me to be a girl?" Celeste thought. "After all, there's a streak of gray in her hair, and she's lean as a cat. It's not as if she has a childlike face. She looks as if she's suffered terribly. Poor thing. Even if she is a fraud, I can't help feeling sorry for her. She has a quality of innocence."

Celeste remembered the countess' saying, "The czar's daughters were like hothouse flowers."

"Bluebells, daisies, and violets," Celeste said softly.

"What?"

"Never mind. I was just thinking that you seem rather Victorian."

"My mother was very strict with us. Of course, she was more lenient toward my brother, but he was so ill."

She said this straight out, without a flicker of an eyelid, a hint of laughter, embarrassment, or any sign that she was lying.

Of course, that didn't in itself mean anything. Celeste considered that the girl might be a very accomplished fraud.

Celeste continued to look at that face, Romanov to the bones beneath the skin, and wondered.

"You must believe me," the girl said tremulously. "It took a great deal to get to see you tonight. I had to plan, wait till Madame Kropotkina fell asleep. If she catches me. . . ."

The girl began to shiver. This much at least wasn't pretense. She was terrified.

"All right. Tell me your story, and I'll do what I can, Tatiana," Celeste said, deciding to use that name for the moment. It fitted like a glove.

"It hurts me to talk about the Revolution. It destroyed everything I loved. When the day came that the Bolsheviks took us to Ekaterinburg, I didn't expect to die. But I wish I had. I wish Sergei had let me die."

"Sergei?"

"He was a member of the Cheka, the secret police. What the Bolsheviks didn't know was that he was a double agent. He was supposed to save all of us, but that was impossible. He chose to save me."

"Why?"

Tatiana shrank into herself. There was pain in her eyes.

"It was luck, merely luck, at first. One morning I was ill and so allowed to rest in my room while my father and sisters went for a walk and my mother remained with Alexis in his room. Sergei had been assigned to watch me. Apparently we all were to be executed that day, but I didn't know it. The Cheka was a professional organization, and its men gave no sign. Sergei knew what was planned, of course, and was trying desperately to free at least one of us. Then he spotted the cleaning woman arriving. He noticed she was about my height and weight. When she came into my room, Sergei stunned her with his gun butt, dragged her into the closet to muffle all sounds, and strangled her. Then he revealed he was on our side."

"And you left your family?"

"I was dazed, stupefied. Sergei told me they were to be rescued later. Otherwise, I would never have gone with him. He told me to put on the dead woman's clothes and not to forget her kerchief. It saved me. If Russian peasant women had gone bareheaded, I would have been shot that day."

"It kept your face hidden."

"Not entirely; it's not a veil. But it helped. And I kept my head down. Fortunately the men of the Cheka trusted Sergei. When he told them that the Grand Duchess Tatiana wanted to take a nap, they believed him, and he was told to join the men who were watching my father and sisters. They took no notice of me. I was just the cleaning woman as far as they were concerned. I left the house, Sergei right behind me. Once outside, he didn't go in search of my father but led me to the high fence surrounding the house. It was very dangerous. There were guards at the gate. But Sergei kept them busy talking, and they scarcely nodded at me as I went by. I walked on. Sergei made some excuse to the guard about leaving the house. It wasn't unusual. The men were always going back and forth into the city. Then he came after me."

"What did you do?"

"We went to the railway station at once, for there wasn't much time. Luckily Sergei's papers were in order, and with all the chaos we were able to reach the border. There Sergei bribed a guard with money raised by the émigrés. I didn't know my family was dead until I reached Ankara. Then I wished I was dead, too."

"And then? How did you live? Did Sergei turn you over to other émigrés?"

The girl shook her head. "I can't remember."

"What?"

Timidly the girl reached out and touched Celeste's arm. "Listen, I know you think that's an excuse for covering blanks in my knowledge, the sort of thing that only an impostor would say. But ask yourself this: Would I make up anything as nonsensical as amnesia? If I were a liar, I'd give you a thousand details, make up a dozen stories that sounded plausible. Understand that it did terrible things to me, seeing Russia in ruins, learning my whole family had been murdered. Amnesia released me from the pain.

Think what it would do to you if you lost everything you'd ever had, lost an entire world."

The girl's words cut Celeste like a knife. She said, "In a very little way I know what you went through. It's more than an abstraction to me anyway."

"Then you do believe me?"

Celeste was hesitant. "I don't know. Have you any idea what happened to Sergei?"

"I don't know. I assume he was shot. The Bolsheviks traced us. I have vague recollections: a dark and twisting alley; a courtyard; an old Moslem woman taking me into her kitchen. After that everything is blank. I think the amnesia helped me survive. There was no need for me to pretend I wasn't the Grand Duchess Tatiana and so slip up in some way. I really didn't know I was."

"But you know now. Who told you?"

Tatiana looked about wildly as if she were afraid somehow she'd be overheard. "Madame Kropotkina," she whispered. "I was living like an Arab urchin, a street beggar, working in kitchens for scraps of food. There was a Frenchwoman living in Cairo, devoted to spiritualism. About five years ago Madame Kropotkina visited her and stepped into the kitchen. She saw me, and she stopped dead, began talking about Russia, questioning me. Then she went away."

"Five years is a long time."

"I didn't see her again for a while, although I'm sure she had her spies. She wanted to make sure I didn't leave Cairo without her knowing. During that time she found out what she could about the execution, the many plots to rescue us. Then she came back. Gave me small amounts of money from time to time, got me a job assisting a mind reader in a cheap nightclub. She showed me pictures of Russia, spoke to me of things that had happened, did everything she could to make me remember."

"And you did, finally."

"Details had come back to me, bits and pieces of things. Then four months ago she came to Cairo for the last time. She showed me a painting of my dear sister

Olga, and everything that had happened came crashing back. I screamed because pain returned with the memory. But Madame K. had a quiet kind of joy about her. She said I was ready."

"Ready for what?"

"To come to Nov and meet the countess. She said there would be no more poverty, no more hunger. I would live royally again."

"And do you?"

"Oh, yes. You should see my room."

"I see. Clearly. Want to know what I think? You are a fake. Some Russian peasant girl or whatever who resembles the dead Tatiana passing yourself off as a grand duchess to get rich. You're not the only one of your kind at Nov. I'm quite sure Nicholas Bazdeev is as eager as you to cheat the countess, but in his case I suspect he wants jewels."

Celeste gasped. The girl was shaking so badly she seemed almost convulsive.

"No, you don't understand. He doesn't want her jewels. It's me he's come for, don't you see?"

"What are you saying?"

"I've been trying to tell you. You say I'm a fake because I want to be here, that I'm using the countess for her money. But I'm not. I don't want her wealth, not a penny. I'd leave here in a minute if they'd only let me."

Celeste gasped.

"I'm being betrayed."

"And you think it's Nicholas."

"I don't know for sure, but I don't trust him."

"You've seen him then. But I thought you were kept hidden."

"Only since you've come. The countess was worried about you because you're an outsider. She doesn't see that the true danger will come to me from Russians."

"Nicholas isn't Russian."

"Are you sure?"

"Positive."

"Oh, no. What am I going to do?"

"Stay calm. I'll think of something. Boris Berg. What do you think of him?"

"He has been kind to me. I know he's tried to persuade the countess to send Madame Kropotkina away."

"Has he now?" Celeste was relieved.

"I fear her most of all," said Tatiana.

Celeste watched the girl closely. There was no question of acting or pretense. Tatiana was scared out of her wits.

Celeste sighed. If the girl were a fraud, then she must be the strangest one ever. An impostor finding herself in danger would confess to her true identity, admit she was a fraud, and prove it. That ought to be easy enough. Everyone has relatives, identification papers, a past. The countess would banish her from Nov at once.

Celeste took in Tatiana's features, that Romanov face.

"Yes, the Soviet government would want you returned. Think what plots could be hatched to get you back to the Russian throne."

"The countess is already busy with them."

"The countess?"

"She's bent on restoring the monarchy. She thinks that within a few years we all could be back in Russia living on our estates again. She's convinced the émigrés will rally around me, and while the Russian people rise in rebellion, England and America will send troops to Russia to fight the Bolsheviks. I shall be wed to a cousin and produce the next czar."

"What a mad idea!" said Celeste.

"The countess is mad."

"Still, I can see where the Russian government would be glad to have you out of the way, especially since they've told the world you died with your family."

"I'm a symbol of so many things."

"Why did you come to me?"

"I heard Countess Ustinova talking about you before you came. You're young; you're an outsider. You were coming here for a good reason. Everyone else is caught up in the entanglements at Nov except you. You're the only person I can turn to."

"Has anyone threatened you yet?"

Tatiana shivered. "Being with Madame Kropotkina is threat enough. She was kind to me in Cairo, but now she's horrible."

"Have you spoken to Countess Ustinova about her?"

"I don't dare. Madame K. is clever. She'd find out. Somehow she'd get back at me."

"What can I do, Tatiana?"

"Protect me from Madame Kropotkina and whoever else wants to hurt me. It could be anybody, you see, anybody greedy. I'm trapped at Nov. I can't get away. Anybody could get in touch with the Bolsheviks and help them find a way to get in here and kidnap or kill me. It would be easier here than in Cairo. So please get me away from Madame Kropotkina. Come and stay with me in my room. Be my friend. I need a friend desperately."

A friend. "I've never had friends," Celeste said. "My father and I didn't live that way. I've always been alone, and now I'm more alone than ever."

The glitter of the palaces of Old Russia came back to Celeste. To be friends with a grand duchess. It was quite an honor.

The opening of the door took them by surprise. They both stared at the woman who filled the doorway.

"What are you doing here?" Madame Kropotkina growled at Tatiana.

The grand duchess whimpered.

"What did you say to her?"

"I told Celeste my real name."

Madame Kropotkina roared and struck Tatiana a blow on the side of her head that sent her reeling.

"Stop it!" Celeste shouted, incensed. "You have no right to hit Tatiana Romanova. I'll tell your sister."

Madame K. made a visible effort to calm down.

"Tell her. She won't believe you. At the moment my sister thinks I'm a saint because I found the grand duchess. So it won't do you any good. I suggest we all try to get along. Life is lived more pleasantly that way."

"I'm tired of being locked in my room," Tatiana whispered.

"Well, you accomplished that much tonight. Since Celeste knows who you are, you can come out of your room."

"And am I then free of Dron?" said Celeste. "He didn't manage to prevent my meeting the grand duchess after all."

"You're an impudent girl. I don't like you. We are just trying to protect Tatiana. We don't know you, what you might do. I have devoted myself to the grand duchess. Cared for her. Kept her fed. Sacrificed myself for her welfare. I even put up with that pet of hers."

"Pet?"

"A cat she found in Egypt. Useless animals, cats." Madame Kropotkina lit a cigarette. "If it weren't for me, Tatiana would be a beggar. She owes me a lot."

Submissively Tatiana bowed her head.

Chapter X

"So you have discovered my secret," the countess said, peering anxiously at Celeste. "Can I trust you?"

They were in the countess' sitting room, drinking the inevitable glass of tea.

"I won't tell anyone outside Nov about the grand duchess. Not anyone."

"I hope you mean that. Even a careless word on your part in a letter could cause disaster."

"I'll be very cautious," Celeste said, thinking ruefully to herself that she had no one to write to.

"If the Bolsheviks get even a hint that she's here, I shudder to think what it would mean. Of course, it would be very hard for them to get an agent inside Nov. That's why my sister brought Tatiana here. Because we can watch out for strangers."

"Or your sister can smuggle them in when she's ready," Celeste thought. Aloud she said, "Countess?"

"Yes?"

"Would it be possible for me to move in with the grand duchess?" At the look of horror on the countess' face Celeste rushed on. "It's hard for her to spend all her time with someone your sister's age. She needs a companion, a friend."

"The grand duchess doesn't always know what's in her best interest. She's been hurt deeply by the events of her life, and they've clouded her judgment."

"Yes, but I know you want her to be happy."

"I cherish her. She is my finest treasure. And I treat her as such. Therefore, I want to keep her safe."

"But you can trust me, Countess. Besides, I've had a chance to speak with her again today."

"So I heard. You spent the morning together."

"I do think she'd prefer to spend her time with me, rather than Madame K."

"You've been listening to gossip about my sister. Understand, Celeste, my sister has made many mistakes. At times I've been quite angry with her myself. But I won't believe some of the things said about her, quite frightful things. She's been very conscientious where the grand duchess is concerned. So consider the subject closed. Though I hate to part with it, here, you may have your Easter egg again. Then I'd go see Boris Berg if I were you. Time you got your mind back on your studies."

Boris, using a jeweler's eyepiece, was contemplating a black opal. When Celeste entered the study, he nodded curtly. The opal in his hand flashed a bright and to Celeste angry streak of red as if the jewel had caught his mood.

Afraid to antagonize him, Celeste bent her head over a Fabergé cigarette case of royal blue enamel on gold with a snake made of diamonds curved across its surface.

"So you couldn't control your curiosity," Boris said.

"The grand duchess came to me."

"You should have sent her away."

Celeste was indignant. "She's the daughter of your czar! How can you say that?"

"I'm not indifferent to her fate. Like all good Russians, I share a deep mystical bond with her."

Celeste remembered how she had once had a glimpse of Boris' room, barren except for a simple cot, a small dresser. But on the wall hung a painting of Nicholas II, and next to it a bronze crucifix.

"I have done what I can to persuade the countess to surround Tatiana with guards rather than leave her to Madame Kropotkina. But she won't listen. So I do what I can. Keep my eyes and ears open. Remain alert. So that I will be ready for the attack."

"Attack?"

"Certainly. I have no doubt the Bolsheviks will try to abduct her. The question is how and when. What a tragedy it would be if they succeeded. The countess has great plans for the grand duchess."

"Boris, you don't mean to tell me that you believe in this incredible scheme to restore the Romanovs to power."

"It is not so very long since the Revolution. Perhaps there is a chance." Boris cried exultantly, "I would go to my death to see her crowned."

"You're like all the others here. She's nothing but a symbol to you. To me she's a human being, one who's suffered terribly. She wants me to stay with her, be her friend."

Boris began pacing the room. "Are you insane? You have no bond with her as I have, no strands of history bringing you together. Stay away from her. When the Bolsheviks come for her, anyone who stands in their way will be hurt."

Celeste stared at him. He was so upset, so worried. Did she dare get her hopes up? Did he love her?

He dashed her hopes to the ground immediately. "It is as your teacher and mentor that I speak to you," he explained. "You have become in a small way my responsibility. I don't want you to do anything foolish or reckless."

"Oh." Celeste looked away. Then she said, "I've always sought protection for myself one way or another. Just this once I'm willing to help protect someone else. My mind is made up. Would you speak to Countess Ustinova for me? Tell her I'd like to replace Madame Kropotkina as companion to the grand duchess, become, how shall I put it, Tatiana's lady-in-waiting."

"My talking to her will do you absolutely no good. Not that I would do it under any circumstances. Anyway, it should be obvious to you by now that only one person here can influence the countess significantly."

"Not Princess Xenia.'"

Boris laughed. "Don't be silly. I mean Nicholas Bazdeev."

"Nicholas!" Celeste cried. "Oh, no. I couldn't ask him." She recalled the fear that had crossed Tatiana's face at the very thought of him.

"Good. Then you won't get near the grand duchess, and I won't have to worry about you."

Celeste was ashamed of herself. The first difficulty and she was already backing off.

"I'll speak to him," she said assertively, trying to sound brave, "but only when the right moment comes."

It came for Celeste on a magnificent day when for all the cold the sun was a disk of hammered gold in a sky blue as springtime. Despite their romance with Old Russia, the émigrés preferred to stay indoors near a deliciously hot stove. But Celeste felt she would smother if she didn't leave the great house for a while and breathe fresh air.

But where to go? She stepped outside. Newly plowed trails led everywhere: toward the woods, the peasants' houses, the church. She decided on the church. Although the countess went there regularly in her sleigh, Celeste had not yet been inside it.

She moved quickly, boots crunching in the snow. Peasants hauling wood lowered their eyes as she passed, for with that special walk of hers and the rich sable fur coat she'd borrowed from Tatiana, she looked like a royal princess.

The church was everything she wanted it to be. She admired the icons on the walls, brightly colored primitive painting of saints and holy men. The priest, an old man with a white beard, saw her and shuffled toward her. But he spoke only Russian, and after a moment of awkwardness between them he turned and left her.

Celeste wondered what he did with himself all day here in this distant outpost of the great Russian Orthodox Church. She'd been told that he was an archbishop and that he'd lived in Moscow. Did he miss St. Basil's, the huge church with a rainbow of onion-shaped domes?

Someone entered the church and came up to her. "Taking a day away from Fabergé?" he asked.

It was Nicholas.

She felt a sinking sensation.

"I came out for a walk."

"So did I. But then I often do. Have to escape sometimes."

He glanced at the sable coat, the boots, the warm hat Celeste wore. "If you're finished with the church, come along."

She wanted to say no, to hang back, but she didn't dare. He slipped his arm through hers, and they went out together into the cold, strong air.

"Still resisting me?" he said, for he could feel the tension she communicated right through the heavy fur of her coat.

"I might not," she said, forcing herself to be pleasing, "if you did me a favor."

"What's this? You come to me for something, not Boris Berg?"

"He can't help me. You can." Quickly she told him. Begged him to talk to the countess, bring her around. And all the time she was thinking that she might be asking help from the very person who planned to destroy her friend.

He looked at her steadily. "Come with me," he said, and began moving quickly, pulling her along.

"Where are we going?" she asked.

"To a place where we can keep warm and have a little chat."

They reached the peasant village and stopped before one of the isbas, a log cabin slightly isolated from the rest.

"Whose house is this?"

"Dron's," Nicholas answered.

"He frightens me. I don't want to go inside."

"But that's precisely where you're going." Nicholas pushed Celeste onto the ladder leading to the door high above the snow level. "Anyway, he's not here. He rarely is. He has a room of his own near the kitchens at the manor house."

Nicholas followed Celeste into the large single room that formed the complete interior of the house. He drew a bench up to the side of the enormous earthen stove with a mattress on top where Dron slept when he stayed at the isba. Celeste got as far away from Nicholas as she could, standing near "the beautiful corner," where Dron, like all the peasants, kept religious objects. Icons hung above a row of unlit candles.

"You're playing games with me," he snapped. "No matter what I do for you, it won't change your mind. You'll still pine for Boris." He watched her, brooding. "I'm not a fool, Celeste."

"No, you aren't. Very well, I won't be silly or coy. Please do as I ask just because it's me making the request."

A shaft of light from one of the small windows caught him, highlighted his satanic handsomeness. Dress him in black velvet with white lace at the cuffs, hand him a cutlass, and he'd be Captain Kidd to the life.

He gave some thought to what she'd said. Then he answered, "I'll do my best with the countess. You have my word."

She tried to look as if his word meant something. And failed.

In frustration he brought his fist down hard against the edge of the bench and gave a roar as if he meant to smash up Dron's isba.

"You're convinced you can rely on Boris, but not on me. Yet you've never put him to the test. I'm tired of this. I told you I knew something about him you wouldn't want to hear. Well, here it is."

Celeste covered her ears, tried to block Nicholas' words out.

But Nicholas shouted, "He's engaged."

"No, he can't be! I suspected there might be a woman somewhere, but I never dreamed of anything as serious as marriage. Why did you tell me, Nicholas? You've broken my heart. Now I won't even be able to dream."

"About him? Good. Maybe you'll start dreaming about me."

"Who is the woman?" Celeste asked miserably.

"A Russian. What would you expect? Xenia got the whole story out of the countess. Xenia's very good at sniffing things out. The woman's name is Vera Rasnikova. She's trapped inside Russia, but she gets letters through to Boris from time to time. He's salting away all his money because he thinks he can buy her freedom if he earns enough."

"But he can't have seen her for years if she's still in Russia. I don't understand."

"He was betrothed to her in childhood. His parents chose her for him."

"But that's absurd and archaic. He needn't feel obliged to marry her now."

"Perhaps he loves her. Anyway this is just the sort of engagement Boris would want—all duty and no joy."

Celeste began to cry. Nicholas went up to her, wiped away the pebble of a tear with his glove.

"So you see, Celeste," he said tenderly, "one of these days you will have to forget him. I'll be waiting for you."

"Never," Celeste thought and saw right through the tenderness. He was still a man she could easily imagine trading the Grand Duchess Tatiana Romanova to her enemies for gold, silver, or—it was an inescapable image—doubloons and pieces of eight.

Chapter XI

Tatiana and Celeste went into dinner together. Men rose to bow, women to curtsy. When they were seated again, Celeste understood why her friend's face was haggard and strained.

Beneath their superficial reverence the émigrés eyed the grand duchess as if she were a jewel for sale on the open market. Indeed, she looked a bit like one, for the countess saw to it that she was dressed like an empress.

Diamonds glittered at Tatiana's throat, ears, and wrists, blazed on the buckles of her shoes. She'd been put on display, her presence required at every party and banquet. Although she was amazingly regal, Celeste knew what it cost Tatiana to face the émigrés every day.

Tatiana could never tell if the sparkle in Prince Stolypin's eyes was a sparkle of greed or what lurked behind Madame Vladimira's innocent smile. Poverty had made the émigrés lethal and dangerous.

Madame Kropotkina was eating her soup loudly and splashingly. Staring at Tatiana, she said harshly, "So I am to lose you."

Tatiana's voice when she answered was very soft. "I don't understand."

"I have been told by my sister that I am to move my things out of your room."

Celeste and Tatiana exchanged looks of surprise, then of triumph. Nicholas had done it! Not overnight, of course, it had taken him weeks, but he'd kept his word.

"I don't like the idea." Madame Kropotkina bit brutishly into a piece of bread. "Tossed aside after all I've done."

"Hush, Natalia, the decision is made," said the countess coldly.

"What magic you have, *chéri*," Xenia murmured to Nicholas. He glanced at her with his usual arrogance but didn't answer.

"You'll still need looking after, Tatiana, and I don't intend to stop. I'll bring you a bowl of borscht from time to time. It will make you strong."

"Yes, madame," Tatiana said woodenly.

"And I'll see that your pillow's plumped and your tea cooled a little just the way you like it."

"Servants can do that," the countess said.

"It isn't the same, Helene. I don't want Tatiana to think she's losing me. You wouldn't want that, would you, my little Grand Duchess? You need me."

Tatiana nodded passively as if she hadn't the energy to combat Madame Kropotkina. Hadn't the will to put her in her place.

"She's so terrified of the woman it's made her vulnerable. Good thing I'm here," Celeste thought.

Madame Kropotkina didn't say another word for the rest of the meal. She just sat stuffing herself, smearing food into her mouth with grimy fingers. Within minutes her scarlet dress, almost phosphorescent in its brightness, was badly stained.

"Hideous woman," Celeste thought, and saw aversion on the faces of everyone else in the room. But those bulging eyes didn't even blink. Madame Kropotkina brooded there, a force, a presence, like some huge, malignant mother hen.

"This," said Tatiana the next morning, "is my room."

Celeste felt faint. She did not walk so much as stumble into the room behind the servants bearing her possessions.

"Oh, Tatiana, the countess has let her fantasies run rampant." But had she? Celeste felt again that strange sense of an alien world, inscrutable and exotic.

"It was like this in our great palaces. But our private apartments were decorated simply. My mother was the granddaughter of Queen Victoria, Celeste. She preferred chintz."

Chintz! "Your mother must have felt out of her element in Russia. This room looks as if"—Celeste sought for the right words—"as if it were blown to Nov on the winds of Samarkand."

Beneath Celeste's feet was a rug so Persian it might have been a magic carpet. The walls of the room were marble and hung with green silk. Velvet of a darker green had been used to upholster the divans and chairs. All the tables, large and small, were covered with carpets on which stood vases of hard porcelain, colored rose and *gros bleu.*

Celeste looked up at the ceiling and marveled. Elaborately gilded, it formed a rounded dome, which glowed in the light of lamps of pink glass and crystal. Alabaster busts of the Romanov czars glowered at Celeste from all parts of the room. Here was Nicholas II's father, a man so strong he could bend iron bars. There was Czar Alexander, the liberator who had freed the serfs. Catherine the Great, Peter the Great, Ivan the Good, and, mouth twisted in contempt, the face of the fierce and vicious Ivan the Terrible.

Celeste gave a start and whirled around to see more innocent objects, evidence of Fabergé's genius: little jeweled apes clustered about crystal flowers; shining storks on long golden legs, attended by quartz peasants. Looking at her solemnly was one little jade bear.

"Remind you of Boris?" Tatiana asked, for by now she knew how much Celeste loved him.

Celeste touched the bear softly, then went on, walking about. She reached out to feel the spun gold tassels hanging from the drapes and the pearl-beaded coverlet of the great hand-carved wooden bed. A small gilded bed for Celeste had been placed not far from it.

Servants had removed the bed Madame Kropotkina

had slept in, to Celeste's profound relief. Anything of Madame K.'s seemed contaminated.

Overcome by the opulence of the room, she sat down on a divan decorated with perfumed cushions worthy of a Turkish harem. Something buried in the cushions growled.

"What's this? Oh, Tatiana. I think I've just met Catiche."

A cat as beautiful as any Celeste had ever seen burrowed its way from under the cushions. It had thick, short steel blue fur tinged with silver, and its eyes were a fiery green.

"So this is your Russian Blue. Fancy finding a cat like this in Egypt."

"She used to come to the nightclub for scraps. I don't know who owned her. But she lived like a stray. That's why I took her in. She was just like me. Living the same life."

"She's a perfect jewel," said Celeste. As if the cat, too, were royal, it wore a jeweled collar, a gift of the countess. Circling its neck was a band of gold studded with the best of the lesser gems: topaz, aquamarine, beryl, moonstone, and citrine. All it needed were earrings of lapiz lazuli to achieve the stature of an Egyptian cat.

Celeste stroked Catiche, then looked around the room sadly. "How inadequate my things seem in this splendid room, rather like poor orphans herded into a grand cathedral."

"But not the Easter egg," said Tatiana. "That belongs here."

"Does seeing it upset you?" Celeste asked anxiously.

Tatiana was on the verge of tears, but she shook her head bravely. "It's beautiful, and it was Mama's." She opened the pearl-handled doors and cried, "My sisters, my brother, if only they were here."

Celeste went to her friend, soothed and comforted her. "Be thankful you had a happy childhood, Tatiana. Some people never know any happiness at all. And don't blame yourself because they died and you lived. They loved you. They would have wanted you to get away."

"We were so close. I never wanted to leave them, not even for a day. And now I'm alone. Do you know, I even used to worry about getting married someday. My sisters and I had a secret club. We called ourselves OTMA. It's an acronym for the first initials of our names. Olga, Tatiana, Marie, Anastasia. We vowed never to separate."

"In a sense you didn't. They live on inside you, in your memory. And you never have to marry. No one need replace them."

"Countess Ustinova will force me to marry. That is, if I survive."

"Tatiana, don't say that. I'm here now. You're not facing Nov alone."

"How different it all could have been. I might be queen of England today or empress of Germany if there hadn't been war and revolution."

"Yes, your father would have been able to choose, wouldn't he, from the full sweep of royal houses?" In her mind Celeste saw a long path strewn with glittering crowns.

"It would have been better to have married any of them, even a mad king or a decadent prince, than to have starved as I have. But to have remained with my family in Old Russia, that would have been best."

"Happiness is rare, Tatiana."

"You never speak much about your father, Celeste," Tatiana said curiously.

Sadly Celeste said, "It's painful to talk about him. How can I describe what life was like with him? Rather like being a diamond in his lapel, nothing more."

"Poor Celeste."

"He was charming and handsome but completely selfish. Acted as if he owned the world and everyone in it."

"My Uncle Gregory was like that. He was always at the center of a scandal."

"Over women?"

"Yes. He had a dacha in the mountains of Kirghiz near China where he brought ballerinas. And he used to take world tours. He gambled; he drank. Took up with one mistress after another. Mama tried to keep the stories from our ears. But eventually we heard them. I liked him, but then I saw only his charming side. He brought us candies and dolls, and besides, he was quite an elegant man. Always meticulous. He set the fashion, he and the Prince of Wales. No one wore clothes with more style than Gregory Romanov."

"I've heard about the pearls he gave to Madame Oupenskaya."

"That was a mistake. He spent far too much money on them. There was a terrible furor." Mournfully Tatiana said, "It was another nail in my father's coffin."

"Oh, Tatiana, I wish I could give you the Easter egg since it belonged to your mother. But I need it."

"And I wish I could give you my cat," Tatiana said, "since you are lonely. But I need her."

Catiche pricked up her ears and ran nimbly to the door.

Tatiana and Celeste exchanged looks.

"Perhaps," Tatiana whispered, "there is someone out there."

Celeste crossed the room almost as silently as a cat.

She listened. Nothing. Then she opened the door a crack. And found herself staring into the burning eyes of Dron.

"I thought I was finished with him," Celeste cried.

Tatiana rushed forward and spoke to him in Russian. He answered her, and she seemed to age as he spoke. She shut the door.

"Oh, Celeste, he's been posted to guard us. To follow me and watch me all the time."

"What?"

"It seems that's the only way the countess would agree to letting you stay with me. She thinks Madame Kropotkina was capable of protecting me but that you can't."

"Oh, Tatiana, how awful! What will we do?"

"I don't know, Celeste. I am afraid, too. The countess believes that by standing there, he keeps others out. But what if, Celeste, his real intention is to keep us shut in here waiting for whoever will come?"

Celeste didn't scream. But she wanted to very much.

Chapter XII

"He's always there, always with her. At night sometimes I wake to hear him snoring. He's dozed off in a chair that blocks the door. But if I so much as put my foot on the ground, he wakes up."

Boris stared at her impassively. "Would you prefer Madame Kropotkina? Dron is there to protect the grand duchess."

"Oh, don't be so blind," Celeste protested. "During the day Tatiana's practically shackled to him. It's making her tense and even unhappier than before."

"The countess has chosen Dron," Boris said, and turned his attention to a tray made of lapis lazuli and trimmed with peridots that Fabergé had designed at the turn of the century.

"Well, if the countess is so fond of Tatiana, then she ought to consider what she's doing to the girl. Take tonight."

"The New Year's Ball?"

"Yes. I'm terribly afraid it will provide the perfect opportunity for someone to try something. The house is so crowded with strangers. Émigrés seem to have come from all over the world. There'll be a lot of confusion. You know, Boris, you simply must change your mind and come to the ball. You should be there in case Tatiana needs you."

"I never attend balls. They are foolish. Besides, your suggestion doesn't make any sense. No one will hurt her at the ball. Not with the throng that will be there."

"You never know. I wouldn't put anything past

Madame Kropotkina. She's bold enough to try anything anyplace. She's forever coming to our room, poking about and prying. Badgering Tatiana. The poor girl starts shaking at the sound of the woman's voice. If Dron weren't there, I'm sure she'd eavesdrop on us."

"There, you see. Be thankful for Dron."

Celeste shot Boris a furious look. "And have you noticed Nicholas lately? He's become almost melancholic. He's plotting something."

"Be objective, Celeste. Tonight is the one night you don't have to worry about the grand duchess. Still, I promise I shall watch out for trouble. But then you don't need my promise. I always do."

Celeste began to brood as she stared at him. "You haven't been very pleasant to me lately, Boris. You're so abrupt, so curt."

"You're imagining things," he said calmly.

Celeste wondered if he might not be right. Since she'd heard about Vera Rasnikova, she'd seethed with jealousy. At times she found herself almost baiting Boris, prodding him as if he really were a bear out of a Russian circus.

"Actually it is you who have become rude," he told her pointedly.

She flushed. Perhaps she just couldn't stand his indifference anymore and was reading all kinds of signs and meanings into everything he said and did, giving him emotions, even negative ones, rather than accept his dreary neglect.

"If I've been rude, I apologize, Boris." She looked out the window at the eternal snow. "Perhaps it's the weather. So confining. It's getting to me."

He smiled. "Winter is a small thing to be concerned with. It's a kind season, really, a great leveler. Everywhere you look there is snow. Perhaps you need the Gypsies. Well, you won't have to wait long for them now."

"Are they coming from very far away?"

"Canada. Wisconsin."

"What unromantic places for them."

"Nonsense. They emigrated to Canada because unlike

you, they like the winter. They understand it. Well, of course, many Russians have gone there for generations."

"Are they interesting?"

"The Gypsies?" Boris laughed. "Try the Doukhobors if you want exotic people. They founded a commune in Canada. When they think the government's persecuting them, they go naked and burn down their houses." Boris' eyes twinkled. "And to think they say all the radicals are in Russia."

"But seriously, Boris, are the Gypsies safe?"

"They don't steal horses or babies, if that's what you mean. We had a long tradition of humility and resignation in Russia before the Revolution, and Gypsies are a peaceable lot. They're really meek, like peasants. And peasants are born pacifists."

"Still, I don't like the idea of any more strangers coming here."

"They aren't strangers," Boris said. "They often visited Dron's village."

"Oh, no."

Boris' eyes lost their twinkle. "I understand. You'd wish the grand duchess on the dark side of the moon to keep her safe. You are amazingly loyal." He reached out and patted Celeste's hand. It was an avuncular gesture, but she looked at him lovingly, her lips parted slightly like a flower opening. Abruptly he dropped her hand and turned away, snapping whatever thread of tenderness there had been between them.

"You'd better go," he said gruffly, indicating the pile of work on his desk.

Celeste, unquenchable, asked herself if he wasn't a bit too abrupt for a man who was completely indifferent to her. She knew she'd launched a campaign to make herself irresistible. Was it working at last?

She tried one more time. "Do come tonight, Boris. Nicholas will be there."

"So?"

"He's an adventurer and a fraud."

"So you say, but it is because of him that you are now the grand duchess' companion."

Boris picked up a sheaf of papers and sighed at the laborious tasks ahead. As Celeste watched his shoulders slump under his interminable burden of duty, she decided she had the worst rival in the world: Boris' conscience.

"It isn't fresh peasant prettiness I have to fear," she thought, threading her way past lavender and pink jeweled treasures. "It's Boris' sense of honor. He's given his word to Vera. He'll never go back on it."

Well, at least if she didn't have love, she had friendship. Shared confidences with Tatiana helped prop her up in a dozen ways during the course of a day. Tatiana sensed her moods and attitudes and sympathized.

"It's taken very little time for us to grow so fond of each other," Celeste thought. But that's what loneliness can do, allow a quick intense leap into intimate friendship.

She saw her friend ahead of her, surrounded by fawning émigrés.

"They're destroying her," Celeste thought. "The closer I get to her, the nearer we are in thought and purpose, the more I can see how unhappy she is. She's even lost weight, and she hasn't an ounce to spare."

Celeste went up to her and, speaking softly so the ever-present Dron would at least have to work to hear her, said, "Are you ready for tonight?"

Tatiana smiled, but her eyes were troubled. "I am to officiate again," she said, visibly exhausted, weighed down by an imaginary crown.

The two women had been up late, whispering together. "You ought to take a nap," Celeste said. "How can the countess expect so much of you when she knows you're frail?"

"I don't want to go to my room."

"Why?"

"Because Madame Kropotkina is there." The smile on Tatiana's face was fixed, there only for the benefit of the gaping émigrés.

"Dron, Madame Kropotkina, Nicholas. Enemies everywhere. Even an animal has its lair. But not my friend," Celeste decided as she watched Tatiana. "How formal she is with the émigrés, how marvelously she knows court etiquette. To think I once thought her a peasant pretending to be a grand duchess. Impossible, I have only to watch her to see how graciously Romanov she is. Still, if she keeps going like this, the Bolsheviks won't have to destroy her. She's practically a bag of royal bones. If only she'd stayed in Egypt. . . ."

Worry nibbled at Celeste until the very moment she went to the ball.

"Mademoiselle Celeste Dorchester." A liveried footman announced her. She had never before been inside the grand ballroom since it was truly spectacular, reserved only for the most festive entertainments.

As was customary, she had arrived before the grand duchess, who would make an official entrance later in the evening when all the guests were there.

"How magnificent!" Celeste thought, and for a moment all that was Dorchester in her blotted out her fears as she looked down at the pageantry of a Russian ball. Yet she herself was quite as spectacular, for now that she was the grand duchess' favorite, Countess Ustinova had seen to it that she was dressed to dazzle.

Although the dress she wore was a full two decades out of style, it was still very beautiful. It was the color of true cream. The skirt was long but slit to show the legs. Above it was a tunic with a border of glass beads, and there was also a jeweled belt of charming little colored agates. A darling ermine-trimmed stole completed the costume.

When Celeste had first seen the dress laid delicately across her bed, she'd said, "How lovely and how Russian, too. Someone looking very beautiful wore it to see *Scheherazade* or *The Firebird*. It's gossamer in my hands. But at midnight on New Year's it will be 1928, and oh, I want to welcome in the new, not celebrate the old."

Still, standing there at the top of the stairs, she was a vision, the soft cream-colored dress giving her beauty a dreamlike touch. Everyone who saw her was moved as if they were staring at a living jewel.

Aging émigrés filled the crowd, so Celeste's eyes went straight to Nicholas, who, in an officer's uniform of green and scarlet, shone like the sun because of his youth. He saw Celeste, too. Then her feet could not carry her fast enough down the carpeted stairs to lose herself in the crowd. He was too attractive. To hide from him, Celeste wedged herself behind the potted palms which lined the huge silver mirrors of the ballroom. She peeked out at the émigrés from her jungle of palms and watched them dance, while above their heads chandeliers of gold and crystal rained diamonds of light over everyone. Tall columns of jasper and malachite as superb as those in the Winter Palace dwarfed the dancers but could not compete for color.

All the men wore the brilliant uniforms of the White Army decorated in gold braid. On each man's chest glittered a dozen medals, which made the effect all the more dazzling. The women wore brocades and satins, and some carried delicate ivory fans. Around their shoulders were fine cashmere shawls in pink and lilac. Most wore headdresses of pearls and Bulgarian silver. A few even wore light silken veils in the Turkish style.

In their own eyes age had fled at least for this one night, and every woman was radiantly happy.

"Yet how macabre," Celeste thought, "how terribly wrong, that this ballroom isn't filled with beautiful girls and dashing young men." She imagined the orchestra vanishing, with Death alone piping the tune, a skeleton in imperial robes.

But the peasant musicians struck up a polonaise, and the image of death vanished as Celeste felt a keen urge to dance. She moved forward and watched the couples circling the smoothly polished wooden floor. An old man dressed as a Hussar officer saw her, put his arms around her, and away they went. Celeste had as much natural grace as the ballerinas he'd admired when he was young. He imagined to himself that he was dancing with one now and wished only that he could reach into his pocket for a trinket to give her, a citrine brooch or a crystal egg, as in the old days.

When the dance was over, she didn't slip back among the palms but kept herself in view. And soon she was swept up into a mazurka. After that she went on dancing. A long line formed. She waltzed with an émigré in a Cossack's uniform. Spinning, she had a brief glimpse of a winter scene through a window. Then she was spun around again into the light of the ballroom, where summer smiled.

A huge table that ran the length of the ballroom was set for the midnight feast to welcome New Year's in the style of Old Russia, which meant according to the Julian calendar. They would dine on lobster salad served on plates of gold. Drink Zonka, sugar doused with cognac, wine, and spices. They would eat fruits brought up from the tropics, while outside, the stars seemed flecks of ice and the wind whistled coldly.

Celeste was whirled past a figure dressed in black jet. It was Xenia, standing alone. Her eyes had a wicked shine.

"She's excited about something," Celeste thought. "And that frightens me. Her greed's almost palpable. Where is Nicholas? Where is Tatiana? I know something awful will happen tonight as surely as if I had a sixth sense."

A new partner took hold of Celeste. By now her cheeks were coral from exertion, and she was growing dizzy. Around she went again and again until she saw a blur of green and scarlet and found herself gliding in the arms of someone young and strong.

"Nicholas," she whispered, and the orchestra began to play a waltz. Before she could say no and tear herself away, he had her floating beautifully, her whole body a graceful tribute to the glory of a waltz. He was a wonderful dancer, and everyone stopped to watch them.

They were the perfect couple, matching hand in glove. Celeste fought it, but in the end she gave herself to the moment, closed her eyes, and whirled one-two-three, one-two-three. She dreamed that she was dancing on a lake of dark clouds. Then she opened her eyes, and light came cascading down, streaming like golden treasure around Nicholas' handsome piratical face.

"Admit you love me," he said simply. "Go on," he pressed. "Admit it."

Confused, she stared at him. Then she caught a glimpse of twinkling blackness which was not part of any dream: Xenia. "Tatiana, what was I thinking of?" She thought. "Forgive me, but just for a moment waltzing made me as drunk as champagne."

Abruptly, discordantly the music stopped. Celeste felt as if ice water had been poured on her. She stepped back. So did Nicholas, though in his case with reluctance. He didn't want to let her go.

"He's not brooding about anything tonight," Celeste realized. "He's got a kind of nervous energy about him, just like Xenia."

There was a fanfare of music. Celeste turned, saw Tatiana coming down the stairs, dressed in cloth of silver, her train carried by Dron. Everyone bowed or curtsied low.

When Celeste rose, she saw that Nicholas had gone off to join Xenia. The two had their heads together and were whispering like conspirators.

"Conspirators," Celeste told herself with dread, "so pent up they might explode."

Chapter XIII

The émigrés waited patiently until the grand duchess was seated in a chair gilded like a throne. Now was the moment for Tatiana to nod to the orchestra so they could play once more. But she made no gesture in their direction; she merely sat still, a thin doll in an oversized chair.

"What's the matter?" Celeste thought, taking in the shadows under her friend's eyes, the mouth crumpling with fatigue.

The émigrés began to whisper, then to talk. An air of expectancy hung over them, of curiosity and concern.

Then the countess clapped her hands. "My friends," she cried, "they have arrived!"

"They?" Celeste wondered.

The émigrés knew. Their voices rose. They bubbled with laughter.

Then on cue a band of Gypsies burst into the ballroom. Strumming balalaikas, shaking tambourines, they raced down the ballroom stairs with such vigor they quite took Celeste's breath away.

"So that's it, Gypsies," she thought to herself, scrutinizing them.

Prince Stolypin cried out that he was back in Old Russia at last.

"I don't trust them at all," Celeste decided as they roared past her like the wind. "They're wild, more primitive even than peasants. They're like a natural force."

But the émigrés appreciated them, roaring with delight. For the first time that night Celeste saw Madame Kropotkina. She seemed to fly out of nowhere to give the

Gypsies mammoth hugs, to stroke their cheeks and murmur to them.

Dron, too, grabbed their hands as the Gypsies went by with a skip and a hop.

Celeste tried to reach Tatiana, but a slew of servants got in her way, bringing in platters of Russian food for the Gypsies: fine caviar, smoked meats, and thick black breads.

Suddenly Celeste found herself pushed back into the crowd which fringed the dance floor as the floor was cleared for the Gypsies. She listened to the oohs and ahs, all deserved, for how the Gypsies played and danced, putting heart and soul into their music. The women leaped, their gorgeous dresses of red and green ablaze, their earrings of gold glittering in the light of the chandeliers.

The men flailed wildly, driving themselves to higher kicks, to greater abandonment and glory. One of the young Gypsies, handsome and dark, looked like the hero of an operetta. He flashed by Celeste, dazzling the émigrés with his skill and gaiety. He wore a bold red wool peasant blouse, tied with a gay green belt, and he danced proudly, grandly, in trousers tight as breeches, magnificently embroidered in blue and gold thread.

Suddenly he saw Celeste. His face changed. A kind of wonder came to it. He began to perform for her alone, dancing as if his life depended on it, twirling, somersaulting, and, as the music rose, dipping into a kazatsky. Arms folded, kicking his legs, he kept a perfect balance.

"He reminds me of Nicholas," Celeste thought. "I see the same arrogance. Oh, why is it always that sort of man who wants me?"

At that moment she looked up and saw Boris hurrying down the stairs. "He's come to see the Gypsies, not me," she thought. "I couldn't lure him into the ball. Now where are Nicholas and Xenia? They seem to have disappeared. Oh, there they are, leaning against a pillar. How earnestly they're talking. Nicholas looks very intense." Celeste edged through the crowd.

"Perhaps I can eavesdrop without being seen," she thought.

But suddenly the wild dance was over, replaced by the sound of a violin, sentimental and haunting. The whole ballroom was hypnotized by a young Gypsy woman, her eyes black with sorrow.

The woman sang in Romany. Was hers a song of thwarted love, as so many Gypsy ballads are? Celeste couldn't know, but the sound of the woman's voice was irresistible, and the song took Celeste to the heavy snows of Russia. She found herself thinking of campfires in the taiga. The scene was so vivid she could feel the wind on her face and imagine the bright stars above the treetops. She could even taste the vodka which, like fire, warded off the cold.

Celeste looked at Boris clear across the ballroom, and the pain that went through her bit to the heart. He was beyond her reach. She had experienced nothing in comparison to him. He didn't even see the Gypsy woman anymore. Her voice had carried him away to the smell of a Russian pine forest, to the shine of silver birches. He tasted the bread his grandmother used to bake, saw a book of his father's open upon a table, and caught a glimpse of a broad winter sky.

The gulf between Boris and Celeste had never seemed so wide, their differences so clear. He had a home, even if he was exiled from it, a physical place that was specifically his, in his blood. There was nothing substantial in her past. Her entire heritage was tinsel. Change the cities, change the views, grand hotels are all the same.

Doubt came to her, and she wondered whether they could ever be happy together even if she could make him love her. Perhaps she ought to let the dream of him go. But what then? Take up with a Gypsy or a pirate. A dangerous, treacherous pirate at that. The song ended. She found her way to the broad and glittering pillar.

She hid behind it as if it were a huge tree. She could barely hear Xenia and Nicholas on the other side, but she didn't dare show herself. People kept pushing around her, and she tried to look as if she were resting against the pillar just because she was a little drunk.

"Are you ready, *chéri*?"

"Completely."

"You are marvelous at moments like this. I don't know any man who's half as bold. We think alike, you and I."

"Perhaps. But I suspect I'm more selfish, Xenia."

"Because of Anatole? Well, I do need the money for his sake. I want him to be secure more than I want anything. And I want to see to that myself. Can you understand? I don't want him dependent on Countess Ustinova. I hate the way she lords it over all of us that she's the rich one." Xenia sighed. "But I must admit, beyond Anatole I yearn for money for myself, too, gobs of it."

"Spelling indulgence in rich gold letters," Nicholas murmured.

"And I suppose you are doing this only for the adventure?"

"Lower your voice."

"Why? Dancing Gypsies make a lot of noise. Besides, lovers often whisper together in corners, *chéri*. No one will suspect of us of anything more. Who knows, perhaps later tonight you and I will be toasting a triumph? What time do you go to her room?"

Noise clanged as a group of Gypsies dressed as mummers drew near, drowning out Nicholas and Xenia.

A tremor went through Celeste. She slipped past the Gypsies, whose eyes were slits behind masks cut from tree bark.

"I must save Tatiana, but how?" Celeste thought. She bumped into a mummer doing a comic dance. He leered at her. "Boris. I'll talk to Boris."

Celeste searched for him. She spied him out by his size, while the Gypsies drank vodka and the émigrés drank champagne. A Gypsy spirit was taking hold in the ballroom. The mood turned from festive to raucous.

Stripping time away, the émigrés forgot they were old. They flirted and snatched love behind pillars and posts. Countess Ustinova, a little shocked, looked on in a daze, but they were beyond caring about her. They cavorted with the Gypsies.

"This is as it used to be," an old general shouted. "Do you remember, Ilya, your apartment in Moscow and the Gypsy parties we had there? The time we threw a dancing bear out of the window?"

The music turned discordant. The sickening scent of Turkish tobacco hung over everything. Celeste's head began to ache. Through the smoke she saw Madame Kropotkina laughing for all she was worth as she danced with a young Gypsy. Her arms were so tight around him she seemed to be choking him. His eyes bulged. He gasped like a fish. Around and around they went in the same circle like dolls revolving on a music box.

As she pushed her way through the crowd, Celeste was jostled by a Gypsy woman in a mask. With a cry she found herself thrown against Boris.

Startled, he looked down at her. She wasted no time. "Quick," she said, "I've got to talk to you."

"I can barely hear you; it's so noisy in here." Moodily he added, "The ball's degenerating into a Gypsy romp. I've never seen the Gypsies so wild before. I can't imagine what's gotten into them."

"Never mind them. Listen to me."

He bent down, and she stood on tiptoe. Carefully she repeated what Nicholas and Xenia had said.

He growled like an angry bear. "Are you sure?"

"Of every word. Oh, Boris, what are we going to do?"

Desperately Boris looked around the ballroom, his mind turning, seizing on every option, each likely plan. "I'll take the grand duchess to the study in secret and keep her there."

"But how will you get her away from Dron?"

"I don't know," he said grimly.

Just then there came a loud shout from the Gypsies.

"What's happening?" Celeste cried as knots of émigrés began pushing their way between herself and Boris.

"Of course," Boris shouted. "I'd forgotten."

"Forgotten what? I don't understand. I'm growing confused."

"Follow the Gypsies, Celeste. They're leaving the ballroom."

"Leaving?" Then she saw the Gypsies dash up the stairs.

"It is the custom," Boris called, and it was the last Celeste heard from him before the crowd carried her off. Soon she was on the stairs herself. She caught one final glimpse of Tatiana in the gilded chair, the countess on one side, Dron hovering over the other. She tried to catch Tatiana's attention, to signal to her somehow, but it was impossible. Celeste was dragged off by the merrily singing throng.

So loud was the balalaika music that it floated out onto the dark night. The winds carried the music beyond the house all the way to the isbas in the village.

Celeste spotted Madame Vladimira. "Why have we left the ballroom?" she called.

The answer came but not from Madame Vladimira.

The crowd was pressing against Celeste violently now. Old faces stared at her, seemed to mock her. She felt as if she were drowning in an ancient sea. She needed room; she needed air. She twisted around. And felt the scratch of dry, withered skin as a pack of elderly drones penned her in.

She got free, stumbled, and found herself falling against a huge, cushioned mound of flesh.

"Madame Kropotkina!"

"So it is you," Madame Kropotkina said.

"Why did we leave the ballroom?" Celeste asked, her head awhirl. "What is the point of leaving it when everyone at Nov was there?"

"Everyone? Oh, surely not. My dear child, that shows how very little you know about Russian life."

"Now what did that mean. Who else could be here?" Celeste thought to herself. Did the countess keep the metropolitan of Moscow hidden in a secret room? "Perhaps we're reliving the time of the troubles, and I'm on my way to resurrect Boris Godunov and crown him czar. Nothing is too incredible for Nov."

She tramped on with the others to whatever ritual or rendezvous awaited them.

The village was awake and stirring.

Chapter XIV

The doors to the kitchen region were flung open. There in a row, gaping, were cooks, maids, laundresses, and the countess' French chef in a rotund hat the color of flour.

"Why, the Gypsies have come to entertain the servants, that's all. Nothing more mysterious than that," Celeste realized.

A minute later and people were spilling over into laundry rooms and storage chambers. Liveried footmen, blackamoors with shoes that curled at the tips, all the servants in the house were converging on the kitchens. Then the peasants—bearded men and kerchiefed women—came pouring in from the village.

The Gypsies danced for all they were worth. The kitchens grew steamy hot, and one of the peasants produced a flask of vodka and began passing it around.

"Drunk, the whole lot of them," Celeste thought as the crowd surged forward, tossing her into the arms of the fat chef. He sighed at the sight of her and signaled to the crowd to move back, then flung Celeste about in a mad, whirling dance until she felt she was being pounded into a meat pudding.

Then, as if he'd thrown chilled champagne at her, she saw what this gathering meant.

Practically the entire upstairs was deserted, its halls emptied of servants. It was a golden moment to kidnap or kill Tatiana.

But before Celeste could do anything, the crowd surged forward, the chef receded. The Gypsies led the way upstairs.

"Let me pass," Celeste said to a grizzled émigré blocking her way at the head of the stairs. "I have to find someone." Then she saw people putting on coats.

"What's this?" she asked.

"It's a Gypsy tradition to dance in the snow. Cools the blood," the émigré answered. "You there, peasant, before you fall on your face from drink, lend this girl your coat. You've enough vodka in your veins to keep you warm."

"I can't go outside," Celeste howled, but her voice was lost in a great shout, and she was thrust into the night. Despite her fears, the first blast of cold hit her as gloriously refreshing.

Under the bright moon and glittering stars the Gypsies danced frantically. The winter night drove them to yet wilder revels. Kicking their legs high in the air, they shouted fervently, sang with fresh gusto.

The émigrés sang, too, and it was all mad and magical, a scene from the *Nutcracker* ballet. A stage set for the sugar plum fairy or a troup of warrior mice.

Suddenly leaping into view came Dron! He was alone. Tatiana was nowhere in sight.

Dron was drunk, and his eyes were flooded with moonlight. Mumbling in Russian, he whirled ecstatically with the Gypsies and gazed up wondrously at the stars. Flakes of ice were in his beard, and he looked like old Father Frost calling the earth to winter.

Celeste weaved her way through the crowd, her heart pounding. She reached the edge and, skirting it, at last began walking as best she could through an unplowed stretch of snow.

There was no charm to the cold now. It was horrible, and she stumbled and fell in the vast white ocean surrounding her. By the time she got back to the house her feet were numb and she felt half-frozen. She looked up at the warm melting glow of the windows, then went inside.

It was not a mansion peopled by ghosts now. It was a mansion from which all ghosts had fled.

She hurried to the study. It was ominously quiet.

Carefully Celeste put her hand on the doorknob.

The door was opened with a rush from the other side. There, standing in the room, was Boris.

"Is Tatiana safe?" Celeste shouted.

"She's sitting right there." Boris pointed.

Tatiana rose. Celeste caught her.

"Celeste, my friend," Tatiana cried. Like sisters, the two women embraced. Celeste clung gratefully to the slight form.

"It's a good thing I remembered that the Gypsies would dance in the snow," said Boris. "The peasants are quite superstitious about it. They think dancing with the Gypsies protects against the evil eye."

"But how did you manage to slip away with Tatiana?" Celeste asked.

"I saw the countess was disgusted by the behavior of the émigrés, and I knew she wanted the merest excuse to leave the ballroom."

"So he came up to me, Celeste, and told me in a whisper to pretend I was ill," said Tatiana. "The countess told Dron to take me back to my room, and she went off to her sitting room to sulk."

"Over the vulgarity of her émigrés." Boris shook his head critically. "Next, I saw to it that Dron had plenty of vodka to drink, and I spoke to him in Russian about the old days in his village. When I thought he was ready, I told him I'd see Tatiana safely to her room so he could dance with the Gypsies. He knows the countess trusts me. so he went off and left the grand duchess in my care."

"How resourceful Boris is," Celeste thought. "If only I could tell him so, but I don't dare. I might let show how much I love him." So she said only, "Now what?"

"We can't stay here much longer," Boris said, frowning. "Everyone will be coming back to the house to watch the countess toss silver coins to the Gypsies, and we might be discovered."

"Silver coins? But I thought she was angry?"

"She won't sulk long, Celeste. Over and over she forgives her émigrés their faults. Why don't you go upstairs and keep an eye on your room? I'll keep Tatiana in mine until it seems safe for her to go back. Only remember, Celeste, be careful."

Shivering, Celeste made her way upstairs to the deserted corridor with its imperial bedroom. She hid in a broom closet until she heard a drunken voice singing in Russian. She recognized the voice. It was Dron's.

When the singing stopped, Celeste slipped quietly back into the hall, then peered around the corner. Clumsily Dron was trying to maneuver himself into a chair wedged against the door of her room.

He had taken Boris at his word. "He thinks Tatiana's inside. If he were sober, he'd wonder why Boris would have left her unguarded. But he's too drunk to think clearly," Celeste thought.

Dron sat down. He began to snore. He'd fallen asleep.

Celeste took one step forward and froze. Someone was coming up the stairs. Like a shot, she rounded the corner and hid again. Finally, she peeked around the corner again.

What she saw was terrifying.

Nicholas stood over the sleeping peasant. In Nicholas' hand was a heavy wooden candlestick which might have come from Dron's very own "beautiful corner." While Celeste watched in horror, Nicholas brought the candlestick crashing down against Dron's head.

Dron made a strange grunting noise and fell off the chair.

Nicholas stepped over him and cautiously, like the intruder he was, went into Tatiana's room.

Celeste took one last look at the body sprawled on the floor. "Now, you've done it, Nicholas," she thought. "You've killed a man!"

Celeste didn't waste another minute. She ran, as silently as she could, back to Boris.

Chapter XV

Boris bent over the body, nudged it with his foot, rolled it over. Then, gesturing to Tatiana and Celeste to keep back, he entered the grand duchess' room. There was a loud mewing noise, and the door opened again.

Catiche came scampering out. The door stayed open. Both women gazed into the blackened room, wondering who would emerge: Boris or Nicholas. Celeste had lost her coral luster, had become as drawn and pale as her friend. She was on the verge of a scream.

But it was Boris who flicked on the lights. Nicholas was gone. Nervously Celeste and Tatiana stepped over Dron and joined Boris.

"You'd better get the countess," said Celeste. "Do you think she'll believe me when I tell her it was Nicholas who killed Dron?"

"She won't have to believe you," said Boris flatly. "Dron isn't dead."

"Isn't dead!" cried Tatiana.

"Dron will wake up with a bad headache and a bruise on the side of his head, that's all. He'll have to think of a good lie to explain the bruise to the countess, though."

"Why should he lie?"

"He's supposed to protect the grand duchess, Celeste, not get so drunk he's vulnerable to having his head smashed in." Boris added thoughtfully, "I must admit I'm rather impressed with Nicholas Bazdeev. It takes skill to know precisely how to hit a man so as to stun him, not kill him."

"But you weren't here, Tatiana," said Celeste, "so his skill didn't do him any good."

"This time," Tatiana said mournfully.

In her bedroom Xenia was blowing smoke rings and watching them drift slowly toward a dejected Nicholas, seated across the room from her. The smoke rings broke before they touched him, trapping him in a gray, wispy fog.

"Well, tonight was quite a failure, wasn't it, *chéri?* We aren't exactly sipping champagne." She pointed her glittering cigarette holder at him, sighting him along its length as if it were a gun.

"There'll be other opportunities," he said glumly.

"Just don't wait, too long, *chéri*. Understand?"

Nicholas stood up. "Not much of a New Year, is it?"

"We mustn't become pessimistic. Nineteen twenty-eight is going to see me back on the Riviera and in style."

"Sweet dreams, then, Xenia."

"Oh, I'll have them all right. Float off to sleep imagining myself wrapped in furs."

"Riding in a limousine?"

"And wearing," she said with a sigh, "a diamond as big as the Ritz."

When Nicholas was gone, Xenia went to her dresser. Hidden among her things were newspaper clippings. The same face was pictured on each of them. Nicholas' face.

"No matter how much influence you have with Countess Ustinova, Nicholas, she'll get rid of you in an instant if she sees these," Xenia mused.

Yes, he'd better hurry. She'd hate to lose him, but they didn't have forever. She knew a few impetuous young émigrés driving cabs in Paris who'd gladly take his place.

"Next time, *chéri*, you'd better be prepared to kill. Not just her. But anyone, absolutely anyone, who gets in our way," she thought.

Countess Ustinova lay in bed, staring up at the dark ceiling. What had got into her dear ones tonight?

It was the fault of the Gypsies that the émigrés had behaved badly. She'd never seen the Gypsies so irreverent. But, then, one musn't judge them by the standards reserved for the nobility. "When we get back to Russia I'll see that the next czar keeps a tight rein on them," she thought. "Entertaining as they are, perhaps they should be settled in Siberia. Be good for their souls." The countess sighed. "There will be so many political decisions when we go home."

And she drifted off into a dream of her triumphant arrival in Moscow. There she was, leading the procession of returning émigrés while church bells rang. Near her stood the grand duchess, literally spangled in jewels. A little boy stood at her side, her son. A crown was on his head, Catherine's scepter in his small hand.

The countess rolled over. The church bells rang loudly while everyone prayed thankfully that the years of exile were over. Then they vanished. Everyone disappeared except Tatiana, the key, the center, the linchpin of her plan. The grand duchess went into a spin, whirling around and around, and when she stopped, she'd turned into a jeweled idol, a great diamond of a doll. In her arms was her cat, its eyes two perfect emeralds.

Countess Ustinova moaned in her sleep. Russian agents were seizing the great jeweled doll and taking it away. The countess reached out, tried to rescue her treasure, but darkness fell, deep and ebony, and the countess found her strength ebbing away.

The next morning Tatiana Romanova would not get out of bed. "I'm too frightened to go downstairs. If I see Nicholas, I'll scream."

"I know how you feel. I'm petrified of him, too."

"If only Dron had seen Nicholas attack him."

"He didn't see anything." Celeste went to the door. There in the hall Dron stood as usual. But there was a bandage on his head. Celeste went back to her friend. "Now I'm glad he's here. Glad he'll be following you around today."

Tatiana got out of bed. She began walking about, then curled up on the floor and pressed her face against the green silk covering the marble wall. She looked pale and cold as if winter had somehow crept through the marble to the silk, shriveling her.

"How am I to face everyone? How can I smile and nod and greet my subjects regally after last night?"

"Your hands are cold," Celeste said, rubbing them.

Catiche, with her fur like the nap of a blue rug, came to rest on Tatiana's shoulder, warming her.

"I wish it were summer, Celeste, a summer in my childhood. Olga and I used to go swimming off our yacht."

"Summer? Is there such a thing?"

"Will I live past the winter, Celeste?"

"Of course."

"I used to love the season when I was little. We had sleds at Tsarkoye Selo."

"No such memories for me. All I can recall are the jewels my father used to give his mistresses. They reminded me of candy. Diamonds like mints, ruby cinnamon drops. Black onyx made me think of licorice."

"You are trying to amuse me, Celeste, trying to make me feel less worried."

Celeste sighed.

"But it won't work. I'm scared. Death waited at the Winter Palace. And it is here, too."

"And where is it not?" Tatiana and Celeste heard a jarring voice say. Madame Kropotkina had come to pay a visit.

At the sight of her Tatiana grew so scared she became a wraith, a ghost, a spectral figure in her white satin negligee laced with golden thread.

"Tatiana no longer wears her clothes; they wear her," Celeste thought. "Beneath the spectacular fabrics, the glittering trim, she's fading away." Celeste had the macabre vision of her friend turning invisible in order to survive.

Madame K. in contrast was solidly there, corpulent as ever and bejeweled in cheap rhinestones. She wore a new yellow hood, a bashlyk, which was already stained, smudged, and burned by cigarettes. "What are you doing on the floor, my little Grand Duchess? Are you ill?"

"I'm tired, madame."

"Tired?" The woman shot Celeste a sharp look. "Aren't you taking care of her?"

"I'm doing the best I can, but she needs more rest," Celeste said. "Perhaps if your sister would give her fewer duties. . . ."

"What she needs is me to look after her," Madame K. moved awkwardly toward Tatiana. "Tell me, little angel," she cooed, "did you enjoy the Gypsies last night?"

"Last night was very hard for me," Tatiana whispered, casting a terrified look at Celeste.

"Oh, what could be more fun than Gypsies? What a fine place our Mother Russia is with its many people, its many customs. Bulgars, Turks, Mongols, Armenians. And Gypsies. They should make you feel very nostalgic."

Tenderly Madame Kropotkina patted Tatiana on the head, then cupped her face in her hands and looked at the girl's gaunt face. Tatiana stared back like a little bird hypnotized by a serpent.

"You should go out and get some air. It isn't good for you to stay inside all the time. Come to the window with me. See? There is the Gypsy caravan. Look at the color of those wagons and sleighs. They expect you to honor them today with your presence."

"I can't. No, I can't." Tatiana shook her head violently.

"Just as I thought. Without me you cannot manage. But then once one is sheltered as a child, one can never really stand alone."

"Celeste helps me, madame. Tell her, Celeste, how much you do for me."

"Well, as to that I remain a little skeptical," said Madame Kropotkina brusquely, and the look she gave Celeste was bitter. "Does she keep you occupied, Tatiana? Amused? Remember how I made you laugh with stories about Old Russia, all the delicious scandals the Romanovs suppressed."

Curtly Celeste said, "We manage to find plenty to talk about."

"Oh, so you are the grand duchess' confidante now. How touching." Madame Kropotkina sighed. "Dear Tatiana, I guess there is no place in your life anymore for the woman who freed you from the Cairo slums. Yet you should be grateful to me. Now smile. Show how pleased you are that I'm here. I'll make some tea for you."

"Tea, madame?"

"Yes, little Grand Duchess. Tell Celeste to go away, and we will have a pleasant little chat. For an hour or so we shall be, how do those Bolsheviks put it, good comrades."

"No need to send me away. I'll stay and have tea with you," Celeste said so emphatically that Madame K. laughed.

"Are you afraid I'm going to poison Tatiana?" Her laugh grew louder and louder, poured into every corner, rolled up to the ceiling.

But Celeste was remembering how Madame Kropotkina's husband had died. And this morning she didn't find a joke about murder funny.

Madame K. lowered her bulk onto a divan which was too small for her. "Why not let me join you more often? Participate in all your tête-à-têtes?"

Tatiana and Celeste looked away.

"I see. You don't want me. Tatiana, look at me."

The grand duchess did but in a fluttering kind of way as if her nerves were throbbing and her heart pounding.

Harshly, gratingly Madame Kropotkina said, "I thought that by now, Tatiana, you'd be finished with Celeste. But at the rate you are going you will soon be old friends."

Tatiana lowered her head and stared helplessly at Catiche. She stroked the cat's fur. Catiche held very still, and the circlet of jewels she wore gleamed.

Madame Kropotkina frowned at the cat. "Worthless creature," she said. "Don't let it come near me, or I'll wring its little neck."

Catiche kept her distance.

Chapter XVI

"Stay with me a little longer," the grand duchess pleaded.

"Tatiana, I can't."

Even though it was early in the day, the lamps were lit. They cast a soft gauze like glow over the room and made the beautiful domed ceiling shine as if it were made of polished gold.

"You can't go on this way, Tatiana. You've presided over one party and two dinners since the night of the New Year's Ball, and that was weeks ago. Otherwise, you've kept yourself closeted in this room." Celeste sighed. "And kept me with you most of the time."

"It's frightening to be here alone."

"Then come downstairs with me. Dron and Boris will protect you. Think of the countess. She's very concerned."

"Not concerned, disappointed. She set me up as an idol, a model of perfection. If only she'd give up this insane idea of returning to Russia and let me go. I can't stay here and be hunted down like a bear in the forest. If I do evade Nicholas and Xenia, who will be after me next?"

"Don't give up, Tatiana. We'll outwit all your enemies. Meanwhile, you must breathe. You must live."

"Don't lecture me. Stay with me. Keep me company."

"I can't," Celeste groaned. "I have a lesson with Boris."

"Boris. I wish you didn't love him. Then you'd have more time for me."

There were dark shadows under Tatiana's eyes and lines of suffering in her haggard face. Looking at her, Celeste felt terribly guilty.

"Won't you come with me, Tatiana? Then you won't be alone."

The grand duchess shook her head in despair. "I'll wait here with Catiche. Wait for whatever comes." Feeling wintry and depressed, she gazed out the window, at the eternal snow.

Celeste set out to find Boris, and ran into him at last. A servant with a silver tray was talking to him. Boris lifted an envelope from the tray.

As he studied it, his mood changed. By the time Celeste reached him he was lost in gloom, and he turned away from her as if she were no more than a nuisance, an inconvenience. Hurt, she did her best to hide her tears.

"He's heard from Vera Rasnikova. I'm sure of it," she thought.

Hoping she was wrong, she wandered about the great house. Although all the émigrés who had arrived for the New Year's Ball were long since gone, the Gypsies were still here. Celeste saw Madame Vladimira eulogizing her husband, while a cynical old crone, who belonged in a caravan, not a castle, gazed at her dubiously and nodded. In another room Prince Stolypin played chess with an old general. A peasant in green livery served them tea, and two Gypsies watched.

Celeste walked on, past the sitting room where Countess Ustinova sat lost in grief and worry over Tatiana. She reached a back passage where a maid carrying a large laundry basket went about her work. Celeste was too upset even to see her.

"Please don't let it be Vera he's heard from," she begged silently. "Let Vera vanish. Let her marry someone else."

But when Celeste happened to walk past the study, she saw that the door was open. She glanced inside. Boris was there, a letter in his hand. He stared through Celeste as if she didn't exist and whispered, "Vera," poignantly, leaving Celeste eager to join Tatiana and match her mood to mood, weeping bitterly.

Dron gave Celeste a blunt, impassive look as she swung past him. She flung the door open and let out a small, half-strangled cry.

An old Gypsy woman, older even than the émigrés, was in the room. She was nothing more than a tiny bent creature whom time had wrinkled hideously. But her eyes were clear and shrewd, snapping with life, and she wore dangling golden earrings unchanged since she'd first embedded them in her ears when she was a child of ten.

It was Madame Kropotkina who gave the scene its ultimate bizarreness. She sat in a chair, her body slumped into a shapeless mass. Her eyes were closed, and her face was contorted.

Then Celeste noticed Tatiana, terror-stricken, curled up on the floor.

Celeste shouted, "I have only to scream, and Dron will be in here."

"There is no reason for you to scream," the old woman cried. "Hush, or you'll wake Natalia."

"Wake her?"

"She's in a mediumistic trance," Tatiana moaned, barely above a whisper.

At that Madame Kropotkina's head rolled back, and her eyes opened, almost popping out of her face. She began to gasp. She stretched her arms forward, reaching out toward an invisible form. Then she slumped, and her head fell forward as if she were a huge rag doll. Her body quivered and shook.

A strange luminous substance poured out of her mouth.

"Ectoplasm," the Gypsy said.

To Celeste it looked like cheesecloth, treated with phosphorus. A great tremor went through Madame Kropotkina. She cried out, "Raja Din, where are you?" And answered herself in a deep voice, "Here."

The old Gypsy woman snapped her fingers.

Slowly, as if rising through layers of fog, Madame Kropotkina woke up. Breathing hard, she looked at the Gypsy and said, "Well?"

The old woman leaned back against perfumed cushions. "What you lack in talent you make up in show," she said, frankly, "but I do not think being a medium is for you. You have not yet found your niche."

Madame Kropotkina glanced slyly at Celeste and then laughed.

"You see we are not afraid to reveal how we trick people. I admit I use fake devices at séances: tinkling bells; tables rising in the air. I once had an assistant who used to rap on the table. One rap for yes, two for no. But then of course, the room was kept dark to hide him. And to hide the wires that lowered the little trumpet I blew. By using wires, I didn't have to let go of anyone's hands, and everyone thought a visitor from the 'other side' was making the noise."

The Gypsy woman shook her head. "Trickery!" she said contemptuously. "That is your mistake. You have great force and stamina. Create a cult. Rely on your own personality to achieve your aims, not on bells and silly trappings."

Madame Kropotkina scrutinized the old woman's face. "Perhaps you are right. I am mortally sick of spiritualism. Did you know the Psychical Study Association scoffed at me publicly? Oh, yes, in Cairo. I won't tell you what they said about my control, and here I thought Raja Din quite a plausible invention. India has always fascinated me because, you see, despite everything, I believe in the occult. And of course, I admire you. You're gifted."

The woman looked back through time. "I have had many years to find my way."

"She has talent, too," Madame Kropotkina said, indicating Tatiana.

"Ah, well, but a Romanov. Naturally." The old woman nodded. She turned the bright beam of her eyes on Tatiana. "I foretold what would happen to your family years ago. I saw it in the palm of a great Russian lady when she came to see me at Sevastopol before the Revolution. Calamity was vivid in Madame Oupenskaya's hand."

"Madame Oupenskaya!" Madame K. spit. "If only her pearls had been mine, I would have been rich enough to drop spiritualism long ago."

"She deserved pearls. She was beautiful, Natalia."

"And I wasn't. Ah, but the lovers I had when I was young. Still, none of them gave me pearls." She stared sharply at the old woman. "You never wanted pearls."

"Silver is good enough for me. But then I am a Gypsy. And I have my powers, Natalia. That is a kind of richness." She gazed at Celeste. "Why is such a lovely girl unhappy?"

"There's no magic in reading my mood today," Celeste thought. "It must be obvious."

"You are in love, and the love is not returned," said the Gypsy, speculating.

"Yes," said Celeste. "Oh, I wish I were a thousand miles from here."

Tatiana gasped.

"Don't worry, I won't leave you. I'd never forgive myself if something happened to you. But sometimes I feel as if I'm smashing my head against a brick wall."

Painfully the old woman got up, drew near Celeste. "Let me see your palm."

"No." Celeste snatched her hand away from the old woman.

"Read Tatiana's," Madame Kropotkina said with deceptive gentleness, a hint of sadism running under the softness of her voice.

"I don't want to know my future," Tatiana cried out in alarm, shrinking back.

"What? Read the palm of a Romanov?" the old woman mused. "Is that wise? Tragedy is written in the hands of all the czar's relations. But here, child, I cannot resist. Let me look."

Tatiana sat helpless and numb as the old woman went to her. She raised the girl's hand. "Yes, I recognize your palm. The Romanov hands are distinct, alike. And I never forget the lines of a palm, the shape of fingers I've touched. A face can lie. A hand never."

The old woman dropped Tatiana's hand. "But, no, I won't read closely, after all. I'm afraid of what I'll find."

Paralyzed with fear, the grand duchess began to sob.

Celeste was furious. "Go away, both of you, look what you've done." Desperately she tried to soothe Tatiana. "Don't pay any attention to that old woman," she said when Madame Kropotkina and the Gypsy had left. "No one can see into the future. Not yours, not mine, not Boris'." And Celeste began to cry. She told her friend about the letter from Vera.

"I haven't the strength to forget about Boris, Tatiana. But I've come to curse the day I came to Nov."

Chapter XVII

The sound of the balalaikas was very loud. Countess Ustinova was relieved that the Gypsies were leaving so soon. They'd served their purpose, made everyone cheerful. Well, not quite everyone. Tatiana was still mooning about up there in her room.

And now the Gypsies were arranging their final fling. They were going to have a fair, just as they used to every winter in Russia. The grand duchess ought really to go. It was her duty. Yet she said she was tired. What would her mother, the czarina, think of such slackness, such self-indulgence? Of course, she was frightened, but where was her sense of service?

When it came to choose a husband for her, nothing less than an Alexander Nevsky would do. A hero of mythic proportion who'd overcome her weakness and see to it that she kept strictly to her duties.

At this thought the countess caught herself up sharply. Was she really capable of such disloyalty? How shocking and appalling that she should criticize the grand duchess.

Quickly Countess Ustinova reassured herself that she adored Tatiana. And approved of her utterly. Still, she did wish the grand duchess were just a little more unselfish, a little more devoted to the dream of Old Russia. Sometimes the countess wondered if the grand duchess really cared about restoring the monarchy at all. Or if she even wanted to be at Nov.

But that was unthinkable, blasphemous, treasonable. Countess Ustinova shook her head. Tatiana couldn't possibly be that shallow and insipid.

The countess sighed. Fortunately Dron was here, protecting Tatiana, keeping an eye on her, making sure she didn't do anything stupid like try to leave. After all, the future depended on her.

Well, perhaps the moment had come to be more assertive, to make one last effort to bring the grand duchess to her senses. Do or die, she simply had to make an appearance at the Gypsy fair. There would be no compromise with the ways of Old Russia. Not at Nov.

"It is really unfortunate," the countess told herself, "that it's only an ugly duckling who's flown into our lives when we are so in need of a swan. Oh, if only it had been Olga who'd survived."

"It's well below zero, Celeste."

"I know." Not even the heavy furs the women had on could ward off the cold.

"I wish we hadn't come."

"No, the countess was right to force you to leave the house, Tatiana."

"She made a terrible scene. She yelled; she scolded."

"You couldn't expect her to be patient forever," Celeste said as they trudged along through the paths cleared of snow, with Dron to help them when they tripped. "Besides, the Gypsies are leaving tomorrow. Perhaps you'll feel better once they're gone." And she added to herself, "I know I will. They have a way of coming upon one secretly as if about to pounce."

The sun was low in a sky brilliantly blue, and the wooden stalls the Gypsies had erected along the edge of the lake were bright and colorful. Celeste took a deep breath of the fiercely dry air and considered how old-fashioned, how picturesque the scene was. "We might be back ten years or a hundred," she said to herself.

Peasants and émigrés mingled together at the stalls buying icons and cloth, simple hand-painted jewelry, and Russian crosses. At the sight of Tatiana they all bowed, and the Gypsies knelt in the snow. One old man groveled at her feet.

"Celeste, there's Nicholas and Xenia looking at icons. Let's go back."

Celeste pulled Tatiana closer to Dron. "He won't hurt you now," she said, trying to sound brave. "Still, let's avoid him. Here, we'll stop and watch the scissors grinder."

The scissors grinder was a caricature, the swarthy Gypsy of legend, with a thick black villain's mustache. Dron glanced nervously at him and, mumbling in Russian, tried to draw the grand duchess off to watch a group of peasant women dance merrily in the snow, their bright skirts broad as bells.

Stamping her feet to keep warm and burying her hands in her thick ermine muff, Tatiana let Dron lead her about. They stopped in front of a small wooden puppet theater with the double-headed eagle of the czar painted on it.

The curtain opened. A marionette appeared onstage, a Russian Punchinello ready to do battle with a wooden Moor.

"Petrouchka," Tatiana said, conjuring up her childhood.

The marionettes, shrieking in Russian, beat each other with toy swords until a ballerina in white was lowered awkwardly to the stage. Then Petrouchka lashed out at the Moor furiously. But the Moor hit back. Petrouchka fell, then rose at last only to see the Moor embrace the ballerina. Petrouchka wept.

The puppets brought a wan smile to Tatiana's face.

"It doesn't seem very comic to me," said Celeste. "Poor Petrouchka."

Just then the puppeteer stepped out from behind the stage to take a bow. It was the Gypsy who resembled Nicholas, the one who had danced so beautifully at the New Year's Ball. Celeste had seen him since, of course, but she usually avoided him. The resemblance to Nicholas was too close for comfort. She and Tatiana left, Dron trailing behind.

The snow was turning blue with early twilight when the three of them reached the farthest stall. All the peasants and émigrés had drifted away. Celeste barely noticed. She had eyes only for two people, Nicholas and Xenia, and luckily they weren't anywhere near. Just Dron, casting a long shadow on the snow.

Celeste looked at the house. It seemed far away, clear across the lake with a desert of snow to cross to reach it.

"I can't stand the cold another minute," said Tatiana. "My bones are aching."

That was when Celeste's eyes fell on the scarlet tent. It rested on the snow like a Mongolian yurt, and as the weak rays of the setting sun struck it, they gave it a beckoning glow, as if to call the wandering khans to shelter.

Celeste, Tatiana, and Dron were drawn to it as if it were a star shining in the east. Dron pulled the tent flap aside, and they went in.

There, wrapped in so many layers of wool she looked like a mummy, sat the old Gypsy woman. On a table next to her was a pack of tarot cards and a crystal ball.

"Don't hang back," she said. "Can it be that you are afraid of me? Why, I am too weak to hurt anyone." But the power in her eyes belied her words.

For a moment Celeste was afraid to move. Then she told herself she was being a fool. The old woman was right. What could she do to them? After all, Dron was here, alert and on guard, big as any man at Nov except Boris.

Celeste took a step forward. So did Tatiana. But the old woman was staring past them, impaling Dron on a stare.

He screamed and covered his face.

The old woman chanted in Romany.

"She's put a spell on him, Celeste," Tatiana shouted. "He thinks she's got the evil eye."

Then Dron, the strong man, let out a cry of terror and burst from the tent. He would have fought like a wolf against any man, but he couldn't fight magic. Visions of the Rusalki, brutal water spirits, and of the murdering Polodnitsa streamed through his brain and sent him running blindly, madly, across the darkening snows.

Celeste and Tatiana hurled themselves toward the tent opening. But two Gypsies rushed in. One was the scissors grinder. The other was the puppeteer.

"Let me go. Tatiana, oh, Tatiana," Celeste screamed. Then the cloth soaked in chloroform came down over her face, and she plunged into blackness.

Chapter XVIII

First, there was motion. Then there was music, which turned out to be the jingle of bells. Next, leafless trees bowed with snow caught stars in their branches. And finally, there was the shock of icy air.

Celeste was in a sleigh, blankets tucked around her. A stream of silver moonlight showed her that she was not alone. Tatiana, asleep, was huddled beside her.

Celeste tried very hard to think. Where had she been all day? How had she got here? But thinking only made her head ache. So she stopped torturing herself with questions.

A spray of snow flew from under the horses' hooves. A whip cracked in the silence of the night. She settled back, her face a pearl against the darkness of the blankets and the extraordinary whiteness of virgin snow under the moon. Studying the back of the man driving the sleigh, she recognized him: Nicholas.

How audacious of him to do this, steal her away. But why was he taking Tatiana? Well, never mind. He was a Dorchester dream. Celeste sighed over the dark romance of Nicholas. Perhaps they were fabled lovers in a Russian fairy tale. She stared at the moon, losing herself in its beauty until its gold was reflected in her eyes. Yes, that was it, she was a Russian princess eloping in the night. Then the man driving the sleigh turned his head and glanced down at her. The stars dusted him with light.

He wasn't Nicholas! Celeste was shocked. But memories came in a flood, wrenching her sickeningly out of her dream. She was being kidnapped by the Gypsies. And Nicholas wasn't her lover. He was a dangerous stranger, the man who had attacked Dron and who perhaps was somehow behind this kidnapping.

Celeste's head was in a spin. The sky had become a merry-go-round, stars circling above her. Or was it Madame Kropotkina's doing? Had she planned it? Totally confused, Celeste moaned until dizziness overwhelmed her and she blacked out again.

Celeste came to slowly, thinking she was present at the building of the Tower of Babel. There were voices speaking, a mix of foreign tongues. What she saw when she gained full consciousness was almost as incredible as that ancient biblical event.

She was in an abandoned Wisconsin farmhouse, with the wind roaring across the open prairie. Moonlight shone through broken windows. Floorboards buckled, and the walls sagged. It was a thoroughly American relic in prosaic American farm country.

Yet she lay on the floor, bound hand and foot, under a pile of blankets, with Tatiana roped and tied beside her. And gazing at her somberly was a mob of European Gypsies.

So incongruous were they the idea came to Celcste that this was nothing more than a scene in a play with the house a stage and the prairie a backdrop, a painted curtain. But the show was not a comedy. The Gypsy women had harsh expressions on their faces, and the men held very sharp knives.

Every Gypsy who'd been at Nov was there, and through cracks in the wall Celeste could see a line of sleighs and wagons. The caravan was ready to take the nomads wandering again.

Like actors, they parted neatly and let the old Gypsy woman move to the center of the stage. She looked down at Tatiana.

"This is where we leave you, Grand Duchess. But it won't be long before they come for you."

"They?"

"Three Soviet agents. They should be on their way from the railroad station by now."

"How could you do it?" cried Celeste, fury drowning her fear. "Betray the daughter of your czar."

"If it's riches you want, the countess will give you money if you set me free," said Tatiana.

"Don't turn us over to Soviet agents. Think what they'll do to us," begged Celeste.

"What happens to you is unimportant. You have made the mistake of getting in the way. However, the grand duchess is another matter. I regret what must be done to her."

"Then change your mind. It's not too late. Let us go," Celeste said. "The countess—"

"The countess can't give me what I want. I look into my own future, and what do I see? Blackness. There are very few years left me. I want to spend those years in Russia. I want to go home."

A leadenness came over Celeste. She looked at Tatiana and saw how frightened she was, a little mouse trembling.

"It has been a long exile," said the old Gypsy woman. "So when Russian agents came to me in Canada, I said yes, I would help them kidnap the grand duchess. They knew we Gypsies could get inside Nov and they couldn't."

"What a neat trade," Celeste said angrily. "You give them Tatiana, and they let you return to Russia."

The old woman smiled. "We are all going home at last, the rest of my tribe to live and me to die." She raised her hand, and all the Gypsies bowed mockingly to Tatiana. Then they vanished.

Horses neighed. There was a rush and stir as the caravan started up. Soon there was no sound save the wind tearing furiously at the old abandoned house.

"If only you'd listened to Boris, Celeste, and kept away from me."

"Hush."

"I should never have sought you out, begged for your

help. But perhaps they won't hurt you. After all, the Bolsheviks have no quarrel with you. Maybe they'll let you go."

"Do you really believe that?"

Tatiana shook her head sadly.

"Neither do I. But we mustn't lie here like sheep waiting to be slaughtered. Shake off your covers. See if you can roll yourself over. Maybe we can find a sharp piece of metal or a shard of glass on the floor and somehow cut these ropes."

"I'm too cold to shake off the covers," Tatiana cried, alarmed.

"All right, I'll do it." It was painfully hard, but Celeste managed to squirm her way out from under the blankets.

"I'll ignore the cold," she told herself idiotically, for it was impossible, and with a Herculean effort she rolled over. But the icy wind blasted her viciously. She lay still.

"You've stopped moving. What's wrong?"

"I can't get any further. And I can't get back. Scream, Tatiana. Scream as loud as you can. Perhaps somehow someone will hear us. Otherwise, I'll never live long enough to be taken by the Bolsheviks. I'll freeze to death first."

Tatiana opened her mouth and wailed. But she was no competition for the wind. It incorporated her scream with its own as it raced across the open land.

Celeste's feet grew numb; her fingers lost all feeling within the thick gloves she wore.

"Stay awake," Tatiana urged desperately.

But Celeste was already drifting off, dreaming of warmth like the frozen little match girl. She imagined that she was in Dron's isba with the candles glowing and the great earthen stove hot. Then she came back to the reality of the winter night. And felt as if she were already a corpse, lying on a slab of ice.

"They'll find me with frost gleaming in my hair and I'll be blue." A vision came to Celeste. Catiche seemed to be with her, purring in sympathy.

But the purr was Tatiana, her voice feeble from the cold, begging Celeste please to stay awake.

"Why should I?" Celeste thought. "I can barely breathe, and my lungs ache. But this is still a better way to die than to be thrown from a train or shot. Or however the Bolsheviks would choose to kill me."

So she stopped resisting, let herself doze off, and the next thing she knew someone was pouring hot brandy down her throat.

Tatiana was murmuring, "Thank God for you, Boris, thank God."

But Celeste was so tired all she could think of was how ironic it was that he should hold her at last just when she was dying. She nestled in his great strong arms and sank toward death.

"He's Vera's; he's Russia's; he'll never be mine," she thought.

Then she realized that someone was telling her she was beautiful, calling her a jewel more fabulous than the rarest diamond. Begging her to wake up and make his somber life glitter with a shining new light.

The words were shafts of life more penetrating than any brandy. She opened her eyes and found that Boris was embracing her clumsily but tenderly.

"Am I dreaming? I wanted you to love me, Boris, but I had no hope. No hope at all."

"Did you think I was blind, Celeste? That first night, when you burst into the study, I thought you were a vision. But I fought against my own feelings. Considered you a temptation sent to torment me. But every time I looked at you I knew I loved you."

"And Vera Rasnikova?"

Boris was startled. "You know of her?"

"Yes. I know you're engaged to be married to a Russian girl."

Troubled, Boris said, "I don't want to talk about her now."

Celeste had hoped he would cry out that the engagement was broken, take her to the old priest in the church at Nov, and marry her tonight. But obviously he had no intention of doing that, and for just a moment the cold of the night returned.

Chapter XIX

Countess Ustinova had aged ten years in one night. The sun was rising weakly over the wintry earth as she sat with Boris, Tatiana, and Celeste in the great house at Nov. The tiled stove baked the air piping hot.

"Whatever you owe Boris, Tatiana, you owe Madame Kropotkina even more."

The misery on the grand duchess' face deepened.

"She was the one who discovered Dron hiding in his isba. I have reprimanded him severely and sent him to work in the kitchen. Five new peasants will guard you from now on, Tatiana. All strong men. There is no chance anyone can hurt you now."

Tatiana shrank from this fresh burden of five jailers instead of one.

"It appears that the Gypsies understood Dron better than I. But then they think the same way peasants do, I suppose. Natalia had a very hard time calming Dron down, making him see that he wasn't suffering from a fatal spell. Imagine! He actually believed he'd be dead by morning. As a result, we had no idea where you'd gone. Certainly I didn't blame the Gypsies for your disappearance any more than I would dear Nicholas or any of the other émigrés. We searched the house, scoured the woods. The peasants even took their pikes and searched the village."

"How did you find us, Boris?" Celeste asked.

"Common sense. It was so bitterly cold I assumed the Gypsies would either set up camp or seek temporary shelter in an isolated place. Well, this is a prosperous region.

There are very few abandoned houses around. I know where they are. I simply set off to explore them."

"You are amazing, Boris."

"When you have roamed the taiga, Celeste, hunted by Bolsheviks, you learn to recognize logical hiding places. I would have continued after the Gypsies once I found you, but I wanted to get you back to Nov."

"Forget them," said the countess. "I certainly shall. When we get back to Russia, the czar will have all Gypsies tortured and publicly hanged."

At these words Tatiana looked down into a deep chasm. She'd had enough of violence and hatred. A vision of freedom came to her, winged like a bird.

But Celeste and Boris barely heard the grand duchess. They were too involved with each other. Later, when they were alone, he kissed her. And she realized the depth of his feeling. His soul seemed to pass into her own so powerfully did he love her.

At last Boris did attend the countess' parties and fetes, but only because Celeste went to them. He even agreed to go to the grand pre-Lenten ball just to see her.

Celeste entered the ballroom, wearing a rose-colored dress trimmed with silver beads and a swansdown stole draped around her shoulders. A spray of flowers designed by Fabergé was pinned to her dress. Once again she oriented herself to malachite and jasper columns, to silver mirrors and palms lush in the wintry north. She wove her way among the émigrés, while above her the chandeliers of gold and crystal spangled her with a magic light.

Boris was standing off to the side, a little apart from the others. He watched, fascinated, as she came toward him.

"I wish I could dance" he said. "But I never learned how."

"It doesn't matter," she said. Immediately she caught sight of Nicholas dancing with Xenia, observed his powerful but elegant style. She remembered the beauty of waltzing with him. But she pushed the memory aside with horror and gave herself over to Boris.

The ballroom was nearly empty, for only the usual émigrés were there. Since the kidnapping the countess had been wary of crowds. So Boris and Celeste had no trouble going off by themselves and finding a quiet corner where lights shimmered privately for them alone.

"I have been thinking, Celeste."

"Yes?" She went taut.

"Marriage is so definite, so final."

"Odd words for you. You're not the man to avoid marriage. I've met that type, thank you. I know it rather well."

"I must have time," he pleaded. "The Rasnikovs were so close to us. Vera's mother was like a sister to mine. All these years Vera has waited for me to free her and marry her. She has no one else. How can I abandon her?"

"Help her leave Russia, Boris, whatever the cost. But marry me. You love me."

"Never have I been so torn in my life. Perhaps we should leave Nov, go off to Italy or Paris. Here I am steeped in Old Russia. I can't think clearly, can't forget the values of a lifetime."

"It would be wonderful to leave. Set up shop in France as Fabergé dealers. I know you'd marry me in time, once you started dreaming about the future instead of the past. But we can't just forget the grand duchess."

"You are loyal to her. Well, I am loyal to Vera."

"Boris, it's not the same. Since the kidnapping Tatiana's been near despair. Not only from fear. There are bars up on our window now and a line of guards forever outside the door. The countess treats her like some sort of jewel in a vault. Well, she's not simply the embodiment of the countess' dream. She's human. If I leave, there'll be no warmth and affection left in her life. Just wardens and jailers."

"Benign ones."

"She's delicate. The countess will destroy her, unintentionally, Boris, for all her lavish gifts. Do you know what Countess Ustinova plans to do? She says the house itself isn't safe enough, so she's going to build a charming little prison cell, a tomb for the living, encrusted with gems. Tatiana will be placed inside. Barbed wire will encircle it, and men with guard dogs will patrol the land around it."

Boris frowned. "When is this to be built?"

"After Easter. And it won't work, Boris. Nicholas will find a way in. I think he's desperate. If so, he'll try something. And even if he fails, I don't know if Tatiana can sustain another shock. As it is, she accuses me of neglecting her for you. As for that, I can't help myself. So you must decide our future here. Though it breaks my heart to say it."

Boris watched her and thought to himself, "Forgive me, Vera, for being human. Still, I mustn't do something I'd regret all my life. I mustn't lose my head."

But vows and promises in the abstract are one thing, and the next morning, as Boris took Celeste out in a sleigh, he wanted to keep her whatever the cost. He had to resist the urge to drive the sleigh on for miles, leave Nov far behind, and head straight for the railroad station.

Holding impulse in check, he guided the sleigh along the side of the lake. The horse trotted briskly, and the sleigh bells rang, bright silver little beehive bells, which broke the winter silence.

"What a cheerful sound they make," Celeste said.

"Everywhere you went in Russia there was the sound of bells. Because there were so many churches, Russia was called 'the land of the bells.' "

Boris cracked his whip smartly, and they went on until they reached a narrow road winding through the woods. It was a mild winter day, and Celeste was warm under the heavy wool blanket which covered her. The cold showed only in her cheeks, which were lustrous, kissed by the frost. Occasionally snow drifting from the branches of trees would powder her dark velvet hood.

Feeling stirred deep within Boris, feeling which had been dead since the terrible days of the Revolution. He'd thought himself immune to love from the time he'd watched the soldiers shoot his father, then turn and beat his mother, kicking her until she was dead.

Celeste had brought him life and a rush of joy and energy. Time had stopped. The world had narrowed until there was only her.

The sound of distant sleigh bells reached them, and the voices of peasants singing in Russian, for another sleigh was coming through the woods. Soon it came into view among the trees. It was filled with men in fur hats and women wearing wool kerchiefs pulled low over their faces, plus shawls to muffle the cold.

They were singing a very old folk song, which Boris remembered well. His mother had sung it to him when he was a child. It was she who had taught him to be responsible. He remembered Vera, and depression settled over him.

It was time to go home. But as Boris took one last look at Celeste, he thought her beautiful. As glorious as the angel in the icon which used to hang above his mother's bed.

Chapter XX

"I wish you would let me plan a real Russian wedding for you," said Countess Ustinova.

"I am not at all certain that there will be any wedding," countered Celeste. She raised her glass of tea. She was in the sitting room again, a silver samovar before her.

"We émigrés have not celebrated a wedding in so long, so very long." And the countess' mind went rolling back to 1917, the central year of her life. "What fabulous ones we have known, though. You should have seen the brides of Old Russia in their white brocade. I had quite an extravagant wedding myself. Exchanged my vows with the count in church, of course, but then I received all my friends and family in a winter garden so large it had twenty hothouse rooms filled with flowers and fruit trees. And why not? Summer brides have the earth covered with flowers for them. Why not winter brides as well?"

"I would be content with a simple wedding," said Celeste, "in any season."

"Winter weddings are very Russian. Well, I don't understand Boris Berg. I don't see what holds him back. He loves you. The whole world can see it."

There was no denying that. Celeste had become the burning obsession of Boris' life, hollowing his cheeks, turning his eyes to ashes. At night he tossed in his bed, thinking of her, falling asleep at dawn only to dream of her.

In the morning he'd look around his austere little room so devoid of personality and think that if Celeste were there, the room would burst into a splendor equal to Tatiana's.

"Still, I must be strong," he'd say. "A man has to be faithful to his ideals."

But he was aware that all his old values were as frail as glass and just might shatter.

Narrowly, taking in every detail, Nicholas watched Xenia put on her makeup. She gazed in the mirror painting youth back into her face as she talked to him.

"I've come to a decision. You have until Easter."

"And that's that? No warmth, no tenderness, no fond memories of the past."

"Oh, come, *chéri,* don't stoop to sentimentality. I don't let my heart govern my brain any more than you do."

Was that true? Nicholas thought of Celeste, how she was like a jewel in the window of Henry Winters' New York store, drawing the eye, making him want to possess her as if she were an emerald ring. But she belonged to Boris now, and there was no way it could have been otherwise. Losing her was the price that had to be paid.

Still, he felt like the passersby who gathered around the window of Henry Winters' store and yearned for priceless treasures only to discover as they brought their hands up that a thick wall of glass prevented them from snatching a prize.

Well, no point in being maudlin. He'd do what he had to no matter how he felt about it.

"Stop feeling sorry for yourself because I'm sending you away," Xenia said. "I've no use for self-pity. Probably because I haven't had the time to indulge it. I spend my time feeling sorry for Anatole."

Nicholas looked at Xenia with respect. He had to admire the way she used all her selfish traits in Anatole's interest, keeping him alive by her ruthlessness, her shrewd intelligence, her cat's talent for landing on her feet.

"I planned the details of the kidnapping," said Nicholas flatly.

"Don't use that to defend yourself. Madame K. had

more of a hand in it than you. That old Gypsy woman confides in her. She and Natalia are friends. What do you know about superstitious peasants and magic spells?"

"Nothing. But I know how to get a caravan started quickly, and I was the one who thought of the farmhouse."

"I wouldn't brag if I were you. Not after that fiasco. Anyway, I've already written your replacement. Unfortunately he can't arrive until after the thaw. After that we can expect drastic results. I know him. He won't hesitate to be as brutal as the situation requires."

"When the time comes," said Nicholas smoothly, "neither will I."

Winter was fading, losing its grip. It had seemed eternal, but that was an illusion, for now it was growing old. The émigrés knew it. Prince Stolypin would doze off and dream about fields of wheat growing in the sun. Madame Vladimira recalled the end of the social season in Petersburg, the return to her estate with its tearful goodbyes, the bustle of moving, the closing up of the house in the city. Others remembered the beautiful white nights of Petersburg, when the sun never set, or the steamy heat of Moscow in August.

Tatiana sat inside her magnificent room and dreamed of hot arid Cairo. She was walking through the slums again, watching boats on the Nile. Then her mind, too, turned to Russia. The image of the Kremlin came to her, and she brooded over it, contemplated its great history and the sweeping power of the czars. At last her mind came to rest on Catherine the Great, the model of all rulers. Tatiana thought about her for a long time.

Madame Kropotkina was prowling the great house at Nov, recalling her lovers. The coming of spring always made her think of crossing the border when she was young and slim and of the Turks she'd met in Istanbul. Or the Frenchmen in Paris. Her favorites, of course, were the Russians who'd come to see her when they traveled through Europe on their grand tours. But that was so long ago now they tended to blur in her memory, and she had trouble differentiating them. All except one.

There was one too special ever to forget.

Celeste, too, sensed that spring was coming. But the mood at Nov was still so frightening she felt she was living on the edge of a cliff. And with it was the misery of seeing things drag on endlessly with Boris. She hadn't felt this insecure since the days when bill collectors had come knocking on the door and her father had gone off to face the world with nothing but a gold-knobbed walking stick and debonair charm.

Each morning she would look out the window to see what sort of day it was, whether there was bright, crackling light or a sky made of snow. Eventually she'd pull away from Tatiana, ignore her plea to stay just a little longer, have one more cup of tea, and Celeste would go off to find Boris.

When the ice on the lake was losing its diamantine hardness, when the snow was softening under penetrating rays of the sun, he said, "The time is coming when I must choose, Celeste. For both our sakes I cannot put it off much longer."

"And what if he decides in favor of her and against me?" Celeste thought, unable to hide her anxiety.

"Perhaps in a new season, when the earth is changed, I'll get a proper perspective on things," Boris said. "Please be patient a little longer."

The winter light caught Celeste, made a halo of her amber hair. He stared at her, fascinated, and whispered, "Just give me till spring. I promise I'll decide by Easter."

From now on she could barely stand the tension, both wanting spring and fearing it. But it was moving inexorably toward Nov. One could smell it in the air, taste it on the wind. And one night, when the stars were like glass in the smooth wall of the sky, Celeste awoke to the sound of water running.

"It's the thaw," Tatiana said. "The snow is melting. Soon I'll be isolated. Put in a cage. Separated even from you. What lies ahead, Celeste? Oh, my good friend, I'm afraid of what the springtime will bring."

"So am I," Celeste said, thinking of Boris and Vera. "Believe me, Tatiana, I am, too."

Chapter XXI

Easter eggs were everywhere. The great house was filled with them, brightly painted or delicately dyed, etched with designs and patterns. Besides real eggs, there were toys, little oval bibelots and curios, made of clear crystal, pretty china, silver that sparkled, and gold that sang. The dining room was cluttered with them. The countess' sitting room was spangled with them. Tatiana's imperial room was made even more sumptuous because of them.

Outside in the starry night everyone, émigrés and peasants alike, walked together around the outside of the rustic wooden church. But Celeste took no joy in the night's ceremony, for by dawn Boris might decide against her.

She walked by his side, contemplating that other Russian Easter she'd known, with its crowds, huge church, and river of candles. This time it was different, the chill night dotted by the merest stream of candles, and she felt it was somehow more authentic than the lavish Easter of a large Russian city. Easter had arrived in just this simple way in villages all across that broad land for generations.

They circled the church. Then the priest led them back to the door. He looked inside, then faced them and shouted, *"Khristos Voskres!"*

"Voistinu Voskrese!" they answered him exultantly.

Celeste surged back into the church with the others and stood in line until it was her turn to kiss the cross. Then she trooped back to the house with the émigrés even though while they were ready for merriment and rejoicing, she felt only detachment and concern.

"I'm a stranger here. Tonight I cannot hide it from myself," she thought, glancing at Boris. "Or from him. How different we are, so very different indeed."

At the house the countess had set up an Easter feast. Celeste watched the émigrés eat rich, creamy pashka and stuff themselves with kulich, the round Easter cake. But she could eat nothing.

She made excuses and went to bed early to fall into a light, unhealthy sleep which went on past Easter sunrise and morning services. By the time she woke up it was past noon.

Tatiana was gone, marched off by Countess Ustinova to receive the émigrés in a formal line as befitted the day. Only Catiche was there, and as Celeste rubbed her cheek against the cat's lustrous fur, Catiche meowed.

"Beautiful thing," Celeste whispered. "Lovely cat, graceful cat. If only it were still winter."

The cat meowed again as if wondering how anyone could prefer winter to this shining Sunday. The sun glowed in the Easter sky with a quiet yellow light, while the air was still crisp enough to allow frost to sparkle like tiny gems of color in the treetops. The lake brimmed with melted snow.

"I can't stand waiting here for Boris. I feel like a prisoner waiting for the executioner to arrive with his ax," Celeste thought.

While Celeste was getting dressed, Tatiana came in. She looked exhausted.

"The Countess said I may rest. Why, what are you doing, putting on your warm coat?"

"I'm too nervous to stay in the house, so I'm going for a long walk."

"Because of Boris," Tatiana said.

"Yes. I've a little calendar inside my mind, and this date is marked on it in black, the color of mourning."

"Oh, Celeste, you can't be sure he'll choose Vera. But

perhaps you should stay here. I'm worried about you. I don't think you should walk alone."

"Why not? I'll go off in the woods. I want solitude, privacy."

"You know, Celeste, Boris isn't really good for you. He's making you over in his own image. You've turned introspective, and you're losing that wonderful aura of glamour that seemed to encase you physically. Forget him, Celeste, before you wind up as gray and somber as he."

"Don't give me advice, Tatiana. What do you know of such things. You've never been in love."

"Don't be cruel."

"I'm sorry." Celeste tied a kerchief of cashmere about her head. "But I must walk."

"When will you be back?"

"Hours from now. After I'm exhausted enough to be able to take any shock."

Once alone, Tatiana felt isolated and frightened again. She looked for Catiche.

"Where are you, kitten? No, no, stop that."

The cat, charmed by the eggs which festooned the room, had found one and was chewing on it.

"Leave it alone. It's made of gold, Catiche."

The cat looked up at her and purred innocently. But when Tatiana's back was turned, Catiche slapped at another egg.

Celeste had been out for barely half an hour when she gave up with a sigh. This was no escape. She was as anxious as ever. Instead of avoiding Boris, perhaps she should find him, have the whole thing out. Better to face the truth than to hide from it.

She returned the way she'd come, her tread heavy, as if the weight of the world were on her shoulders.

The house was abuzz with the voices of émigrés. Celeste looked around hastily, but there was no sign of Boris, and if she went looking for him, the countess would draw her into Easter activities. She couldn't bear that today. Wearily she climbed the stairs. Surely he wouldn't keep her waiting much longer. Certainly he'd come to her soon.

The men guarding the door stepped aside. Still, Celeste paused, for she heard voices. Apparently Tatiana had visitors. Celeste prayed it was Madame Vladimira or Prince Stolypin. Anybody but Madame Kropotkina. Not her. Not today.

She opened the door. A dead silence fell.

Celeste almost fainted.

There was Tatiana, pale and wan. And there, in a skirt of stripes and a blouse of flowers, was the dreaded Madame Kropotkina. But there were two other people in the room besides. A man, dark and piratical. And a woman, blond and glittering.

"Nicholas!" Celeste cried. "Xenia!" She felt a flush of anxious fear. "Why, they're all three leagued against Tatiana. Somehow they've trapped her in her room, and they're going to hurt her," she thought.

But no, Celeste saw instantly how absurd that idea was. There was something about them, an easy relaxation which seemed congenial, friendly. Nicholas was leaning forward as if he and the grand duchess were having a chat. And Xenia was leaning back casually, a cigarette in her hand, a stole draped loosely and comfortably about her shoulders.

Madame Kropotkina, puffing away at a Turkish cigarette, appeared to have settled in for the day. But the scene shifted as Celeste watched. The shock on her face was quickly reflected on theirs. And it hit Celeste like a bomb that the only way these three could have got past the guards at the door was if Tatiana had let them in herself.

Celeste was about to cry out, ask what was going on, but before she could Tatiana shrieked in horror and waved her arms. She pointed to Catiche. "Hurry, Celeste, save your treasure."

Celeste turned her head in time to see Catiche swat her precious Easter egg and knock it to the ground. Spinning around and around, like a red top, it went flying through the air. Then it hit the floor.

For a moment Celeste was so stunned she stood immobilized. Then she rushed to the egg. But it eluded her, went rolling along until with a flying twist it smashed against the wall. She hurried forward. So did the others, but for the moment Celeste was blind to them.

"How badly damaged is it?" Nicholas said. His question went unanswered because the egg went pop and the top came off. Something rolled out. They all were stupefied with amazement. Then all but Celeste were down on their knees, scrambling desperately for the bright object which had spilled out of the hollow egg.

"I've got it," cried Xenia.

"No, I have," said Madame Kropotkina, but it slipped out of her grasp.

"Stop pushing, *chéri*. Keep calm. To think we searched everywhere and never thought of such a hiding place."

Celeste watched them as if through the wrong end of a telescope, for they seemed somehow very far away.

Then Celeste heard Xenia say, "Ah, *chéri*. You've got a firm hold on it. Good. Give it to me. I've waited a long time for this moment. What are you doing?"

Blankly, Celeste watched Nicholas stand up.

Xenia cried, "*Chéri*, have you gone mad?"

"No," said Madame Kropotkina. "He's not mad. But he is in love."

"In love!" Xenia was indignant and disgusted.

Nicholas reached Celeste. She looked up into his dark pirate's face and saw tenderness. Gently he raised her hand. Put something in it. She caught her breath, for she was holding pure magic.

Nicholas had given her the Azov Diamond.

Then Xenia was at her, a whirlwind of raging energy. But Nicholas grabbed Xenia, and clamped his hand across her mouth just as she was about to shriek.

"It's over, Xenia and you're finished. Accept it because it means you're going to need Countess Ustinova's money a little longer. If you scream and bring in the guards, I'll tell her everything. She'll never give you another penny."

Xenia's body went limp in his arms. He let her go.

"You tricked me, *chéri*. You lied to me," she spit, enraged.

"I had to. Otherwise, you would have brought in one of your brutes and Celeste would be dead."

When Celeste heard this, mist filled her mind and her knees buckled. She felt Nicholas' hand on her arm, steadying her.

"Since the first night I saw you at Nov, I've had only two goals," he said. "One was keeping you safe and the other was seeing to it that you got the diamond. You, no one else. I've succeeded, even though I knew I'd have to play the villain and lose you to Boris Berg somewhere along the way."

His words whizzed past Celeste like bullets. She was too dazed to absorb them. "But how did the diamond get into my egg? The Soviets had it under such tight guard in Paris."

"The diamond you saw in Paris, Celeste, was a fake."

Celeste staggered back, clutched the edge of a sofa, and sat down before she collapsed. "But it looked real. So very real."

Madame Kropotkina said, "We were very stubborn, Xenia. Nicholas was right all along."

Nicholas shot her a triumphant glance. "You didn't see Celeste at the exhibition in Paris. I did. I could tell she was dazzled by the gem on display and had no idea it was a sham. But you wouldn't listen to me. You were so sure she had the real diamond here at Nov."

"So she did," said Madame K. "But I can see she's as surprised as we that it was in the egg. Obviously she had no idea where it was hidden. I'm afraid, Xenia, you made some serious miscalculations."

Abruptly Madame K. stopped talking. She glanced at the door.

"Someone's coming," Nicholas whispered. "Quick, Celeste, hide the diamond."

But it was too late. The door had opened, and Boris was staring suspiciously at them.

With an ache Celeste realized that he'd come to tell her whom he'd chosen: Vera or herself. And for a moment in her confused state that seemed far more important than the diamond.

Then he saw the jewel, caught a blast of its fire. The scowl left his face. He was lost in wonder.

"It's mine now, Boris," Celeste said. "I know you don't really care about jewels, but isn't it beautiful?"

Almost timidly he said, "Just let me touch it." He took it from her and examined the gem tenderly, reverently. Then he brought his jeweler's glass out and examined it again.

"It's the Azov Diamond, Boris. It's worth a fortune. We could go off together, you and I. Live any way we pleased."

He let out a sharp sigh and said, "Yes, this is the Azov Diamond, all right. But you're wrong, Celeste. It isn't yours."

"Boris, what are you trying to tell me?"

Gravely he announced, "The Azov Diamond belongs to the Russian people."

The Russian people. Something in the way he said this rang like the bell of doom.

"You will all be quiet, please. Nobody move. Otherwise, I will have to shoot. Not only you but the guards outside the door."

Boris reached inside his jacket and pulled out a gun. He pointed it straight at Celeste's heart.

"I am an agent of the Soviet government," he said. "It is time for me to take our national treasure home."

Chapter XXII

Nicholas forced himself to stay cool, to think rather than to act. Had the gun been pointed at him, he would have leaped at Boris, and the devil take the consequences. But the gun was aimed at Celeste, so he didn't dare move.

Slowly Boris looked around. Took in Xenia sulking and bitter. Madame Kropotkina crossing herself. And Tatiana clinging to her cat.

"How you émigrés disgust me," he said. "I was sent to Nov because it is a center of counterrevolutionary activity, and what do I find? More greed than politics. You are glamorous, Celeste, but you are not like them. I was beginning to sicken here at Nov. Then you came, and it was as if fresh snow had fallen. You affected me so much that when I walked into this room just now, I was on the verge of giving up everything I believed in. Vera Rasnikova had warned me there would be a moment like this in my life."

"Vera?"

"Yes, Celeste. She is my commissar and my dear comrade."

"Your commissar!" said Nicholas.

"She pretended to be my fiancée because it was a convenient way of sending me coded messages. Besides, to a bourgeois mind any letter from a woman means romance. None of the émigrés ever guessed that Vera is simply my boss."

Celeste buried her face in her hands.

"The sight of the diamond had cleared my mind," said Boris. "I love you, Celeste. But what is our love compared to the fate of nations? My country is my life. I must go on working for its interests."

"Put the gun away. You don't need bullets to kill me. Your words are effective enough. Keep the Azov Diamond. I hate it now. It's taking you away from me. I really did hope we'd have a fairy-tale ending, you and I."

Boris glanced quickly at Nicholas. "Take another small step forward like that, and I'll kill her. I must see that the diamond is returned to the Kremlin at all costs even if I lose my own life along the way."

"And what if you do get safely back to Russia?" cried Celeste. "What do you have to look forward to after that?"

"I care nothing for personal happiness. Wherever I'm sent I will go. To the Balkans. To Germany. To Spain."

"Because it is your duty? Oh, Boris."

"Is there a better reason? I am as committed to my dream of humanity as the countess is to her nightmare of serfdom. You are the only lapse from duty I have ever allowed myself. I thought I was immune. Even wealth never tempted me. That's why I was chosen to infiltrate Nov and sent to Amsterdam first to learn about gems. I was incorruptible. Or thought I was, till you."

"I never dreamed you were a spy."

"I never dreamed you were a jewel thief."

"I'm not. Oh, Boris, don't think that of me. The jewel was hidden in my Easter egg. I had no idea it was there."

He grew puzzled. "How strange. There was a rumor in Moscow that the Azov Diamond was a fake, that somehow the real gem had vanished during the Revolution. I find it incomprehensible that it should turn up here at Nov. But I have no time to waste on mysteries. I must leave."

"Why didn't you tell me you were a Soviet agent? Did you think I'd betray you?"

"I didn't dare reveal I was a Bolshevik. Not while I still had work to do here. When I told you I was torn between you and Vera, I meant I was torn between you and Russia. Until I reached a decision one way or the other, I could not say a word. Besides, telling you would have been irresponsible. It would have put you in the kind of danger I face every day of my life. If one of the old generals or Prince Stolypin had the slightest inkling of my true beliefs, he'd order the peasants to kill me. And, you, too, if they saw you as a collaborator."

"To think I chose you, hoping for peace and security."

"My life is filled with violence. But try to understand. I told you my parents were killed in the Revolution. It's true. My father was shot, my mother beaten to death. Do you know who was responsible? The soldiers of the White Army. When my loved ones were killed in the name of the czar, I became a radical."

"I see. Oh, I could forgive you anything. But I can't face losing you. Will I ever see you again?"

He stared down the years ahead. "I don't know. With the world what it is there could be war, turmoil, even desolation. I am destined to go in one direction, you in another."

Celeste wept uncontrollably. "You should have told me the truth and let me face the risks. Who knows? Perhaps I would have been disillusioned and stopped loving you. Then at least I would have been spared this unhappiness. I'm tired of lies. Yours. Nicholas'. Why did you both try to protect me? You should have told me all about the Azov Diamond, Nicholas."

"How could I?" he snapped. "Unless I'd produced it, you wouldn't have believed my story. You didn't trust me."

Celeste stared at him as if struck by a revelation. "No, of course, you're right. I didn't. Nicholas, I got things so twisted."

Then she caught her breath. Boris was watching Madame Kropotkina. From the look on his face she could tell he wanted to shoot the woman.

Contemptuously he said, "You have always struck me as a gross symbol of the aristocracy. You use others. Feed off them. It was your fault Celeste wouldn't even consider leaving Nov. For a while I wanted to go away with her, see if being somewhere else would make a difference in helping me make up my mind. With me or without me she would have been better off out of this poisonous atmosphere."

"Please don't get excited," Madame Kropotkina said nervously.

Boris laughed. "Don't worry. I won't rob you of your contemptible life. But know this. I was onto your game from the beginning. Not that I cared if you robbed your own sister or not. That was your affair."

"I have never robbed Helene," boomed Madame Kropotkina.

"No? Well, what do you call bringing in an imposter and having her pretend to be the Grand Duchess Tatiana Romanova?"

"Imposter!" Celeste swung around and stared at her friend. No, she couldn't be a fraud. That Romanov face.

But Tatiana cried, "Tell everyone. Tell the whole world. I hate playing the grand duchess. The role's made a prisoner of me."

Shock, horror, and a sense of ultimate betrayal washed through Celeste, directed first at the woman she'd thought her friend, then at Boris.

"Why didn't you tell me that much at least?" she said to him. "What was the point of pretending you believed she was really the grand duchess?"

"I warned you to stay away from her at the very beginning," Boris answered. "But you wouldn't listen to me. I assumed that the threats and kidnapping attempt were part of a general plot to deceive Countess Ustinova. After all, if the Russian government was presumably ready to pursue this girl even into the bastion of Nov, then who would think she was a fraud? I knew, of course, that there were no Soviet agents after her, that it was all a fabrication, but only because I am in a position to know. Still, I was very worried about you, Celeste. You'd got yourself in the middle of something involving Princess Xenia and Madame Kropotkina, a dangerous pair. I was afraid you'd get hurt. So I did protect you. But if I'd told you I knew for a fact this woman couldn't be the grand duchess, you would have known at once I was a Soviet spy."

"Why?"

"Dear Celeste, how could I be sure she was a fraud unless I'd seen the real grand duchess' dead body."

"What do you mean?"

"I was at Ekaterinburg the day of the assassination, and I assure you the czar and his entire family are definitely dead."

Everyone was aghast except the false Tatiana. She said, "Perhaps now I'll be allowed to be myself."

"Sonya, you are being naughty." Madame Kropotkina said fiercely, her huge bulk trembling. "Take care or I'll punish you for this outburst. Would you like to feel the birch stick on your back again, little pigeon?"

Sonya put her face in her hands and sobbed, "Don't hurt me, again, Mama. Please don't."

Celeste could barely believe her ears. "You can't mean that Madame Kropotkina is your mother."

Sonya, peeking out from between her fingers like a shy child, whispered, "She is."

In a flash Celeste remembered Madame K.'s overpowering mothering. The way she'd fluffed Sonya's pillows. Brought the girl bowls of borscht. How had she once seemed to Celeste? Why, like a malignant mother hen.

And something else, too, Celeste recalled. A snatch of conversation from the night Sonya had hidden in her room.

Madame K. had surprised them there, or so it seemed. "What did you say to her?" she'd asked the girl named Sonya.

The answer came. "I told Celeste my real name."

And Madame Kropotkina had slapped the girl's face. Not until Celeste had said, "You've no right to hit Tatiana Romanova," had Madame K. calmed down.

"Your real name," Celeste mused, looking at her friend.

"What?"

"Never mind. Just that there were clues I missed. Hints I didn't get. I wanted to believe in you."

"If Madame K. is your mother," said Boris, "then you can't be blamed for what you did. You are a victim."

Sonya gazed at him steadily.

"I pity you," he added, "and I wish you luck. Free yourself. What can be worse than living as you do now? Dearest Celeste, I must leave. Don't forget me."

Her voice trembling Celeste said, "May you get home safely, Boris. Perhaps someday we'll find each other again. After the years have passed, the wars ended, I'll go to Moscow to see the Azov Diamond, and I'll recall how for just a little while it was mine. Maybe you'll be there, too, and we'll meet, gazing at the stone."

He said a final good-bye to her and put his gun away. Calmly he turned his back on them all.

"No," Celeste cried as Nicholas dashed forward. "Let him go."

When the door had clicked shut after Boris, Nicholas said, "But your diamond. . . ."

"I told you I don't want it. It's caused enough harm. Let the Azov Diamond rest in the scepter of Catherine the Great again."

"You imbecile," said Xenia. "How could you just give away such a treasure? You're the very opposite of your father. Nigel spent almost ten years tracking it down."

Celeste, not yet recovered from the last shock, reeled again. "Who told you that?"

"He did. I know a great deal about your father. What he liked to eat. What his favorite colors were. How he adored silk shirts."

Celeste cried out, "Of course, now I know why I disliked you at sight. I thought it was just because you ran so perfectly to type. Only you aren't merely like the women he took as mistresses."

"I am one of those women. His last mistress, to be exact. But I would never have stayed with him if he hadn't promised to make me rich. I didn't like him. He was a cruel man, so different from Anatole. But he didn't want me to go. He was growing tired, you see, though he never let it show, and he didn't want to start all over again with another woman. He was too old. I was a companion, a surrogate wife. His days as a notorious lover were finished. So he bought his comforts by offering me a share of the Azov Diamond. But before he could sell it, he died. And I was as poor as ever."

Madame Kropotkina shook her head. "We were both out of our class, Xenia. I mean, really, the Azov Diamond. It's the impossible dream. We should both have known better than to pursue it. But I never seem to learn. Look at what happened with the pearls."

"The pearls?" asked Xenia.

"The ones Gregory said would come to me. Instead, he gave them to that stupid Oupenskaya woman instead. Well, why are you all staring at me like that? What did you think? That Sonya got that face from a peasant? Why, even the old Gypsy woman could tell when she read her palm that my daughter is a Romanov. Alas, born on the wrong side of the blanket. But she is not so very far from being a grand duchess. After all, her father was a grand duke."

"You and Gregory?" Xenia laughed brutally.

"Don't make fun of me," said Madame Kropotkina ominously.

Xenia stopped laughing.

"Once I was considered a fascinating woman. Men competed for my favors. You look very skeptical, Xenia. But it's true. My love affairs were never trivial. Yours were never anything else."

"Take care," snapped Xenia, "or I'll get even with you, I can be vindictive when I'm provoked."

Nicholas gave her a sharp look. "I hope you're not planning to hurt Celeste. Because I'll see to it that you're very sorry if you do."

Xenia stared at his pirate's face thoughtfully. Then grasping at a few shreds of dignity she said, "I haven't forgotten that I am a princess, not a guttersnipe. Besides, I've no time for petty revenge. I've a fortune to make for

Anatole's sake. Somehow there must be a way. Well, for the moment it's back to Monte. I shall certainly never invite you on another treasure hunt, Nicholas, accomplished thief though you are. But then you can afford to choose love over money. You're so damnably rich."

Chapter XXIII

Madame Kropotkina stood up awkwardly, puffing from the exertion. "Can I go? Boris Berg has had more than enough time to escape. And you have let Xenia go to her room. If you are worried about my being vindictive, well, I am resigned to losing the diamond. I don't fight life the way Xenia does. I am adaptable. But then I've had so many failures. I think they started with Gregory. I fell in love with him in Paris not long after I ran away from my husband. I was young and impressionable. Gregory was marvelous. I have never known anyone like him since. I think of him from time to time. But it is futile to look back. One must think of the future. There's always a new adventure in the offing. Shall we find one, Sonya?"

The girl shook her head. Gathering all her strength, she hurled the word "no" at her mother, probably for the first time in her life.

But Madame Kropotkina met this new resistance with surprising calm. "What is this? A rebellion?" She stared at her daughter calculatingly and lit a cigarette.

Sonya, in contrast, was almost hysterical. "All my life you've bullied me, made me do hateful things. You forced me to pose as Tatiana. Made me read books about the imperial family. Made me memorize so many details about them. You're the one who told me to pretend I'd had amnesia so I wouldn't have to know too much. To you it was like preparing an actress for a part in a play. Yet what we were doing was unscrupulous, wrong. You have no moral sense. How I wish you weren't my mother."

"I took care of you, didn't I, instead of abandoning you at an orphanage?"

"You didn't take care of me. You sent me Cairo to live with strangers."

"I had to keep your birth a secret. My reputation was bad enough. I did not choose to announce publicly that I'd had an illegitimate child. But I paid for nurses to take care of you, and I visited you when I could."

"Oh, Mama, stop it. The only reason you kept me is that I was a link to the Romanovs. You came to see me from time to time so you could make sure I was learning enough about the Russian court. You taught me etiquette, protocol, made me fear you so I'd do what you want. I was a potentially valuable object to you."

As Celeste watched Sonya's painful attempts to assert herself, she realized she couldn't be angry with her. Hadn't Nigel Dorchester been in his own way quite a ruthless parent? And hadn't Celeste allowed herself to be cowed by him? Of course, he'd never been as bizarre, as extreme as Madame K.

"You never let me breathe, you never let me live," Sonya said.

"I was protecting you, providing you with the benefits of a sheltered life. I had to think about the future."

"*Your* future. You used me. But never again will I play a part in any of your schemes to make money. Boris Berg was right. I must free myself."

"To be honest with you, Sonya," said Madame Kropotkina, "I agree."

"What?"

"Yes, I think we should go our separate ways. Unlike Xenia, I always have alternative plans, something in reserve when everything goes crash. And frankly, there is no room for you in my next project. I am going to India."

"Why? What can India offer you?"

"Their religions are very interesting, Sonya. In fact, I am thinking of founding a new religion myself, one in which the ideals of East and West will merge. I think a Russian is eminently suited for that particular task. Lately

I have felt deep mystical stirrings, sensed that there are true gods called Keepers of the Universe who have a message for me. They wish to entrust me with the secret of the art of reincarnation."

"Ah, now I see, Mamma. You're taking the Gypsy woman's advice. Giving up simple tricks in favor of a more subtle form of deception, one based on charisma. It's not the voices of the Keepers of the Universe you hear. It's the call of the silver rupee."

For a fraction of a minute Madame Kropotkina glowered at her daughter. Then she smiled affably. "Ah, well, think what you like. Let's part on good terms. You never know, we may need each other again someday. Now since I've told you my plans, why don't you tell me yours? I hope you don't think you can stay on at Nov. Once Helene learns your real identity she'll order you out."

"I know she'll hate me for deceiving her. Still, she never really liked me, and since I have no intention of trying to stay here, it doesn't matter what she thinks."

"Where are you going?" Madame Kropotkina asked.

"Russia. I've surprised you, Mamma, haven't I? But I'm through with old dreams. And since you have made me so conscious of my Russian heritage, I will embrace the new."

"And what makes you think they'll let you in?"

"You claim I am the daughter of the Grand Duke Gregory Romanov, but there is no way to prove it. I am simply the illegitimate child of a Russian woman whose reputation is unsavory but who is of no political importance whatsoever."

"May I remind you, however, that you are also the niece of Countess Helene Ustinova, who has launched a dozen plots to restore the monarchy."

"Ah, Mamma, that's what will ensure my return. In exchange for letting me live in Russia I'll tell the Bolsheviks everything I know about Nov and its émigrés, down to the last detail. As for how I'll live in Russia, well, you yourself admit I'm a good actress, and Russia has a grea theater."

Madame Kropotkina stared at her daughter with respect. "I don't think I ever appreciated you before." She laughed ironically. "It's a good thing you're not coming with me. In another ten years you might be dominating me."

Madame Kropotkina noticed the small blue-gray cat at her feet.

"I was wrong about you, too, Catiche. You did turn out to be useful. You found the Azov Diamond's hiding place. Too bad you didn't find it sooner, on a day when no one was here but I."

And with a farewell wave Madame Kropotkina set off determined to book passage to India.

As soon as her mother was gone, Sonya fell to her knees beside Celeste. "I ask only one thing before I go, and that is your forgiveness."

"I'm not angry with you. Only there are so many things I still don't understand. It was all a sham, wasn't it? You weren't in any danger. The kidnapping was a kind of play. You know, I sensed that when we were in the abandoned farmhouse. The Gypsies looked as if they were putting on a performance. They seemed like characters on a stage."

"It was all an act put on for your benefit. The whole thing was Xenia's doing really."

Sonya glanced at Nicholas. It was clear that he wanted to be alone with Celeste.

"Nicky will tell you everything. Good-bye, Celeste. Come, Catiche, my little Russian Blue. Home we go."

When Nicholas had Celeste to himself, he slipped his arm around her and tilted her face upward so that he could study it. Reading her mood, he said, "You're in a daze, aren't you?"

"Yes. I still don't understand how my father got hold of the Azov Diamond."

"Your father had many contacts in Russia, not all of them noble. A Finnish engraver got word to him that the Azov Diamond had been smuggled out of Russia. For close to a decade your father tried to track down that jewel. I know," Nicholas added grimly, "because for part of that time I was trying to find it, too."

"You?"

"Yes, but obviously your father had an invaluable piece of information which I lacked and which he never even mentioned to Xenia, and that is that the diamond was hidden inside one of the czarina's Easter eggs. The egg must have passed through the hands of dozens of people who had no idea the pretty trinket contained a fabulous treasure. Too bad your father's persistence didn't pay off. Had he lived to sell the diamond, you would have been rich."

Sadly Celeste said, "I doubt it. He used women. He would probably just have walked out on me. And on Xenia, too."

"Well, it's all speculation now. But by not telling Xenia about the egg, he certainly crossed her up. When she learned after his death that he'd left everything to you, not giving her so much as a sou, she simply assumed you had been given the diamond outright. She figured you'd sell it and keep all the profits. She wouldn't get a thing. So she made up her mind to be clever and steal the diamond from you."

"If she'd only known how little my father confided in me, she would have guessed that I knew nothing about it."

"Yes. Well, when I suggested that possibility to her, she just laughed. She's convinced everyone is as devious as she. That's why my seeing you at the exhibition was so providential. Of course, I didn't know that the woman I fell so dizzyingly in love with on the spot would turn out to be the same woman I'd see again at Nov. But as I told you, I could tell as I watched you in Paris that you believed you were looking at the genuine Azov Diamond. Just imagine my shock that first night at Nov when I found out that Celeste Dorchester, the woman I was supposed to rob and the woman I'd met in Paris, were one and the same. Of course, I realized instantly that your very innocence put you in serious danger because if Xenia didn't get the diamond, it wouldn't be for want of trying and you'd be dead by the time she was finished with you."

"How did she know I was coming here?"

"She kept tabs on you in Paris without your knowing it. When you wrote to the countess asking to come to Nov, Xenia made it her business to be here, too, with a partner. Me. The stage was set for your arrival. But Xenia was only feeling her way, desperately trying to figure out what you'd be like, on the basis of what she'd learned from your father."

"It couldn't have been much."

"There were hints of things. Enough to give her ideas. You see her chief problem was one of method. How could she steal the diamond when she had no idea where it was? She couldn't kill you because then she'd never find it. So she had to trick you into revealing where it was. And to trick you, she had to understand your psychology. She knew that in all probability you'd bring the Azov Diamond with you to Nov. Why else come here if not to avoid the half dozen thieves on the lookout for it in Europe? Thieves, I should add, quite capable of breaking into a vault or safe. Nov is isolated and hardly the sort of place where a stranger bent upon thievery could simply pop up unnoticed. Now it takes time to sell a jewel of the magnitude of the Azov Diamond. Nov would be a very convenient place to wait while a sale was being negotiated."

"What if none of that were true and I'd left the diamond in France?"

"It could still be stolen once Xenia knew where it was. But how precisely was she to get you to tell? She knew you were lonely but aloof, not quick to give affection. If only she could cut through that aloofness. You might confide in a friend, someone you trusted. Xenia didn't think you'd like her simply because she was the sort your father did. And she turned out to be right about that. Then she considered the obvious alternative, a lover. But she knew you were wary of men. Oh, yes, you are, my darling, especially ones who attract you. So whom could she produce who would be both friend to you and informer to us?"

"Sonya."

"She would be here anyway, you see, posing as the grand duchess to get all the money she could from the countess. Xenia knew your father had filled your head with stories about the Russian imperial court. Even if you didn't like Nov, you couldn't help being flattered by the idea of being a favorite of a grand duchess. And if Tatiana was frail, vulnerable, in terrible danger, that made it all the more likely that you'd respond to her sympathetically."

"No wonder Nov felt to me like a court of intrigue. It was."

"But time dragged on. You moved in here with Sonya, spent hours alone with her. Yet you didn't say a word about the diamond. Sonya searched your things and found nothing. Madame Kropotkina berated her for being inept. That's why the poor girl seemed so pale and depressed. Worse yet, you were falling love with Boris Berg. No one had anticipated that. So I was sent to search your room, too, the night of the New Year's Ball."

"What?"

"When you saw me hit Dron, you thought I meant to kidnap Tatiana and turn her over to the Bolsheviks. But I was just getting Dron out of the way so I could look for the diamond. Sonya was supposed to keep you occupied at the ball until I was finished."

"When I overheard you whispering with Xenia, I went to Boris. He took charge of the situation. I really did think you meant to kill her."

"You were supposed to think I was dangerous. It would help strengthen your ties with the grand duchess. But you were so unhappy over Boris by then Xenia decided you might leave Nov. To ensure that you stayed, we contrived the Gypsy kidnapping and made it deliberately dramatic with threats of Soviet agents emerging from the snows. Of course, you weren't meant to go rolling out of your covers, almost freezing to death that night. And we didn't want Boris Berg to discover you. Madame K. was supposed to suggest to the countess that she have all abandoned houses and barns near Nov searched. It's because of what happened between you and Boris that night that Xenia considered the whole kidnapping a fiasco. She was ready to bring in one of her brutal young friends to take my place, which made it vital that I find the diamond for you before it was too late."

"Oh, Nicholas, that someone would be ready to commit murder over a mere stone. But what am I saying? The diamond is so beautiful people have killed before to possess it. I still can't believe there are two diamonds in the world that look so much alike and that both are equally fabulous. The fake must be worth as much as the original."

"The gem you saw at the exhibition in Paris wasn't a diamond at all. It's a quite extraordinary zircon artificially colored by heating."

"A zircon? But surely achieving that deep blue wasn't easy."

"Fabergé's workmen were up to the challenge. It's not surprising they created one of the best imitations in the world."

Chapter XXIV

"What does Fabergé have to do with this?"

"Remember, his son was chosen to sort Russia's great treasures during the Revolution. And the Azov Diamond was the greatest of them all. It's hardly surprising that someone associated with the house of Fabergé conceived the idea of smuggling the stone out of Russia, either for safekeeping or to make a fat profit. Lean days lay ahead for anybody who'd been close to the czar. We'll never know how the switch was made. Only your father apparently had access to that information. Xenia said the Finnish engraver who told him about the diamond was one of Fabergé's craftsmen. Perhaps the 'loyal Bolshevik' overseeing the sorting of the jewels was bribed or fooled. Perhaps one of Fabergé's workers was responsible, perhaps Fabergé's son himself."

"But whoever it was planned enough in advance to allow someone to prepare the zircon as a substitute for the diamond," said Celeste. "What an amazing hoax!"

"Not really. Hoaxes and frauds are as old as the wearing of jewels. And zircons have often been passed off as diamonds. Of all stones only the zircon has the hardness, clarity, color, and brilliant fire to compete with the diamond. Naturally experts can tell the difference, but to identify a zircon, you must examine the back facets through the top of the stone. And for this you need a magnifier. Under a magnifier the facets appear doubled because zircon is a double-refracting substance and diamond is not. But the Russians didn't allow anyone to examine the diamond that closely when it was on display in

Paris. Still, I'm sure they'll be deeply relieved to have the authentic stone back. No matter how good the fake is, it's only a zircon. How can it take the place of Catherine the Great's favorite diamond, the definitive ornament of her scepter? Why, the mysterious history of the Azov Diamond alone would make it precious to the Russians even if it were a smaller, less costly stone."

"But why hide it in the Easter egg?"

"Didn't it ever strike you as odd, Celeste, that your egg has such an obvious and disappointing surprise? After all, Fabergé generally hid his surprises inside the egg, not around the sides. I should have thought of that myself sooner. Then I would have investigated your Easter egg, and maybe I would have discovered it was hollow. But the little doors with the portraits behind them are so charmingly embedded in the egg one doesn't notice that they represent a departure for Fabergé. I suspect the egg was meant to hold a spectacular surprise, but Fabergé had to change his original plan in order to follow the czar's command to economize. Since he'd already created the egg, he simply made certain alterations in its design. Of course, his craftsmen knew that the egg was hollow and that it had a secret mechanism which would release its top, a device common to many of the eggs. When the Bolsheviks confiscated the treasures of the imperial family, the czarina's egg was among them, waiting to be sorted along with Russia's other jewels. Somebody realized what an excellent hiding place it would make and escaped with the Azov Diamond."

"And so the legend grows. Another mysterious story is added."

"Yes. And now that the story's over will you come to New York with me?"

"Please, Nicholas, give me time to get over Boris."

"I'll give you time. But remember, you saw in him what you wanted to see. He would have killed you if he'd had to. He was as ruthless as Xenia when it came to the Azov Diamond."

"But for a better purpose. It won't be easy forgetting

him, but I will try. And though I'm grateful to you, Nicholas, I'm still worried about you." Celeste looked into his handsome pirate's face. "I just can't see myself with a jewel thief."

There was an outburst of noise in the hall, and Countess Ustinova burst in on them. "I have just heard the most shocking news from Xenia. She told me she's quite made up her mind never to take another penny from me, and she's packing her things now. But she said there were a few things I ought to know before she left. Then she looked at me spitefully as if she wanted to hurt me and said the grand duchess is a fake. I'd heard a rumor that my sister had given birth to a child years ago, but one hears so many preposterous things about Natalia it's hard to know what to believe. Not that I'm altogether sorry if it's true. That girl really is not my idea of a grand duchess. I shall be glad to give her and my sister, too, enough money to get as far from Nov as possible. Especially now that a real grand duchess will soon arrive."

Nicholas and Celeste exchanged glances.

"I have proof that the Grand Duchess Anastasia is alive and shares my dream of restoring the monarchy. However, I realize that means nothing to you, Nicholas."

Countess Ustinova waved a sheaf of newspaper clippings which Xenia had given her. "I am deeply hurt and profoundly angry. Look at these gossip columns. And here are pictures of you by the dozen on the society page. You're no Bazdeev. You aren't even Russian. And you can tell your father that I'm finished with him."

"Your father? Tell me," Celeste asked, "what is your real name?"

"Nick Winters."

"Son of Henry Winters, owner of the famous jewelry store in New York," snapped the countess.

At the look on Celeste's face Nicholas laughed.

"Please leave my house, young man, and don't ever come back," shouted Countess Ustinova, and swept out of the room.

"So you see, I'm not a thief, at least not the usual kind.

Occasionally I have helped my father acquire certain rather remarkable stones when unorthodox means were required to obtain them. It's not always the money with me. I went after the Azov Diamond because I wanted it rather the way some men want Rembrandts. And I want you, too."

He looked at her with frank admiration; the amber hair, the cheeks with a pearl's glow, her eyes the color of sapphire.

He smiled. "You'll have the life you deserve, Celeste. Cruises, a penthouse, Paris, whenever you choose. I'm sorry I can't buy you the Azov Diamond, but as you know, it's not for sale. But since you're a jewel among women, I'll see if the Russians will sell me the zircon. Would you settle for Fabergé's glorious fake?"